THE PLANET SPINS ON ITS AXIS, REGARDLESS

The Planet Spins On Its Axis, Regardless

Stories

Kavita A. Jindal

The Planet Spins On Its Axis, Regardless
Copyright © 2025 Kavita A. Jindal
First Edition

All rights reserved. No part of this book may be reproduced or transmitted in any form or by any means, electronic, digital, or mechanical, including photocopy, audio recording, or any information storage and retrieval system, without prior permission from the publisher or author (except by reviewers who may quote brief passages).

This book is a work of fiction. Any references to historical events, real people, or real places are used fictitiously.

Cover art by Jacob Arms

Published by Serving House Books
Lawrence Landing Company
Raleigh, North Carolina 27609
United States of America

www.servinghousebooks.com

Serving House Books is a proud member of

Independent Book Publishers Association
 and
Community of Literary Magazines and Presses

Paperback ISBN: 9781947175716

Library of Congress Control Number: 2025933391

SERVING HOUSE BOOKS

CONTENTS

The Unusual Properties of Cork	1
Three Singers	9
When You Go You Leave A Farce	20
Tulip Persimmon's Head-Wetting	34
Where He Lives	48
Sweet Peas	65
Tipping Point	70
A Flash of Pepper	82
Cocoon Lucky	87
Galvanise Gloss	94
The Afternoon After	99
Shamans in Luburbia	104
Pre-Conception Contracts	111
The Planet Spins On Its Axis, Regardless	129
Acknowledgements	
About the Author	

THE UNUSUAL PROPERTIES OF CORK

Despite what people say about me and the life I led it wasn't often that I travelled distances just to have a special meal. In those days many people prided themselves on being foodies and straying afar just for a unique event.

I did go to north Sweden for a much-hyped dinner which wasn't even for a particular celebration. Afonso Mello had asked me to accompany him. He was the guy I had a smoothie with after my gym session. We both attended the same core workout and then we took our aching butts to the lounge and rested. We had the same bored exercise style. We needed to be kicked and then we treated ourselves to self-care.

The woman Afonso was dating had just broken up with him. He seemed more distraught about the cancellation of an exceptional meal than the disastrous end of his relationship. He'd booked Faviken restaurant six months previously and didn't want to cancel and didn't want to go alone. That's how it happened, and don't tell me that life is predictable. So many things can only be explained in hindsight. In the moment, you just live.

Afonso was a friend, but I'd never had dinner with him. I don't think I was his type of woman. But I didn't know that sort of thing about him, and he certainly didn't know that sort of thing about me. He did ask nicely if I would accompany him. 'Chef Magnus Nilsson', he said, eyes shining at the prospect, as if I would know. I looked it up on DuckDuckGo and saw what a treat it would be. Summer in the Scandinavian countryside, locally grown and hunted ingredients. I had nothing planned for the weekend Afonso had mentioned. A walk by the river. A long walk by the river, singing, if no one was within earshot. But hey, I was footloose and fancy free, and when I checked flight availability and prices, I was happy to give it a shot. That's how I went from London to Sweden one summer weekend.

*

We arrived at Faviken, in the transcendent light of a Nordic evening, having driven for six hours from Stockholm, talking about the scenery enroute and guessing what would be on the menu for dinner. We were shown to our rustic room, as Afonso had decided he was staying on the premises when he'd booked. He didn't want to be driving or taking a taxi to a nearby town after his wine-matched feasting. There was a handful of rooms in the restaurant's own lodgings and they were all the same: two single beds, each hugging a wall, and a woolly rug on the floor between. The ends of our beds hit the small window, round like a porthole, and from it we could spy on the path leading to the restaurant. Our fellow diners were already heading to the patio to gather for drinks. We'd been given the time of 7 p.m. to assemble. Dinner service would start then.

We took turns to dress for dinner. Afonso went ahead, European smart-casual, pale colours, and looking just right. I got in a muddle deciding what to do with my messy hair and so arrived a bit late. I'd settled for a side ponytail tied with a green crushed-velvet scrunchie. My dress was black splashed with yellow irises.

As I stepped onto the veranda, staff began ushering guests into the dining room. They'd been waiting for me. I got the impression that the restaurant ran to a strict schedule. That impression settled into confirmation as the evening wore on. We diners may have been paying big money for a world-famous restaurant and fancyschmancy dishes but we were being treated like schoolchildren. No deviating from what we were expected to do, which, funnily enough, was to follow firm orders. Afonso and the other diners didn't seem to mind, but I found it amusing. I enjoyed disregarding the head waiter's pronouncements. Just occasionally, but enough to irk him.

It also irked Afonso, which wasn't my intention. But then it was probably not Afonso's intention to bore me, but he did. Not with the food, or the magnificent wines, or the restaurant itself, or the whole experience, but with his courteous insistence on answering my silly question: what are you passionate about?

Cork.

He answered so fully between courses, of which there were thirteen, that I had plenty of time to overdrink while I listened. Cork. His family in Portugal farmed it. For generations. I can tell you a lot about cork. It's up to you how much to believe of what I say. It is indestructible, did you know? It is vegan, yes. You can send it to the moon, and aliens will return it to us one day.

Before each course the head waiter clapped his hands so that we could fall silent to hear his pronouncement about the course to be served along with instructions about how to consume it. Which spoon or fork. All in one go or not. Use hands or not. Eat the side with it, after it, before it, or not! I joke not. He told us what we would taste, what we would feel. There was no menu to read and so we had to listen very carefully to what he said. I hissed, 'What? What?' when I heard 'Veal, colt's foot' and 'Colostrum with meadowsweet' and my companion said, 'Shh' and the waitress at our table, gently pouring my wine, admonished, 'No talking just now.' Later I realised how clever this show was. How we strained to hear and pay attention with all our senses. The following day, when we left, we were given the menu but at the time of the announcements I couldn't really be sure what I was hearing. 'What? What?' I said to Afonso when I heard 'Lupin curd gratin' and 'Mahogany clam with beer vinegar' and 'A small egg coated in ash, sauce made from dried trout and pickled marigold'. 'Shh' Afonso said.

Early on I gave up on what I was meant to do and poked my fork rudely into my scallop, *I skalet ur elden* cooked over burning juniper branches. I concentrated on the wines that appeared enchantingly at each course. 'Goodness, Afonso,' I said, between euphoric sips, 'thank you for this, it's *amazing*,' and then I said, 'Tell me more about cork.'

I'm not sure if I was being flippant, but Afonso took me at face-value, which was good of him, and poured out his heart. He missed Portugal and would return there, he said, to his family's bosom when he was done with

The Planet Spins On Its Axis, Regardless

London. He would grow old harvesting the trees that he planted since it took twenty-five years for them to yield. Cork oaks can be harvested every nine years once they're mature. The year of harvest is marked on the trunk so trees don't get harvested by mistake at the wrong time. Cork is a sustainable substance, of course it is! Premium wine corks last fifty years. Fifty. Who keeps wine that long? Well, Afonso's family does.

By dessert, diners were talking across tables to each other, especially the Italian group on one side of us, who winked and sang, and threw questions at us, and then the men made mortified faces like naughty schoolboys when the head-waiter clapped at them. The ladies giggled and after the next course had been duly proclaimed they stage-whispered to me that they were there celebrating a host of events: anniversaries and work promotions.

I felt Afonso grow a bit sad as I got merry with them. There were six delicious desserts, in tiny portions, as if we humans were fragile, earth-loving creatures who didn't over-consume. As if these exquisite bites were what we ate and not five hundred grams of lemon drizzle cake in one sitting. I only talk about me of course. What do I know of the others? From my keepsake menu I can tell you what was served for the sweet end of dinner:

Rhubarb baked in pearl sugar, very fresh cottage cheese

Raspberry Ice

Bone marrow pudding, frozen milk; pickled semi-dried root vegetables

Meat and birch pie

A selection of tar pastilles, meadowsweet candy, dried rowanberries, smoked caramel, sunflower seed nougat, dried blackcurrants

Aromatic seeds; Snus fermented in a used bitters barrel.

That last one was snuff, and I went for it. Afonso delicately declined.

*

When dinner was over and we were allowed to file out into the wondrous light of night, Afonso settled on the patio with a French couple. They were both doctors and their conversation veered towards the rise of curcumin supplements and new discoveries around it. Afonso was enthusiastic, perhaps he could discuss anything at length. I broke in, somewhat nonchalantly, 'Yes, I know all about it. Curcumin is an active ingredient in turmeric. In Ayurveda turmeric has been prescribed for its anti-inflammatory and immune-boosting properties for generations. In fact, in Ayurveda, the ancient Indian medicine system, which you must have heard of,' I gestured to the two physicians, 'we've known about curcumin for five thousand years.'

I clicked my fingers and left them on the veranda. I went into the tepee set up on flat ground opposite. There was a fire burning inside, in the middle. Round benches followed the circle of the tepee and I was beckoned to a cushioned seat by the Italian group who were cheerfully ensconced in there. Their celebrations continued apace as we smoked cigars and knocked back cognacs. Afonso came looking for me at 3 a.m. and in that duskiest hour of the night, we straggled back to our room. I fell into my bed. But too much wine makes me an unruly sleeper, and after I'd wriggled on one side and then the other, I turned towards the other bunk and saw that Afonso was wide awake.

'Oh Afonso, am I a terrible date?'

'No,' he said. He reached across the rug. 'Hold my hand.'

I did. It seemed to soothe him. 'Do you want to sit up and chat?' I didn't add, 'And not about cork trees.'

'Sort of,' he replied. He seemed rather forlorn and I felt that perhaps I had been too merry. I had certainly been accused of that in the past. I went across to him and told him how incredible the experience had been.

'I know,' he said. 'I knew it would be worthwhile. Look at that sky.' He pointed through the porthole. He settled his head on my shoulder and went to sleep in a few minutes, his snores soft and child-like.

I thought I had a glimpse into his soul as I listened to his deep sighing breaths and watched the light outside return to a crisp brightness as it became morning and time for breakfast. Yet more food. Afonso appeared rested but even though I'd scrubbed my face twice and splashed cold water on it, I felt completely groggy. He took my hand as we walked the path to the breakfast terrace, he held my hand on the flight home, and that's when I knew we would remain friends for a very long time, because when Afonso took my hand on that trip he smiled and he was happy, and his genuine happiness put a smile on my face too. I didn't say it, but I also cherished his generous spirit, although aloud I made fun of most of what he had to say.

On the flight back he told me he kept his friends for fifty years.

*

My jokey response to that would come much later. Afonso would, true to his word, call regularly for a chat – he did like to talk – even when he'd returned to Portugal, and had a family and little ones. Fifty years wouldn't pass for Afonso. When he was certain he was dying and had told his friends, I became the one who phoned regularly and who talked more than him, to save him the labour of speech. One of the things I said to him before he died: 'People from India keep their friends for five thousand years. Remember, Afonso? Go laughing, and take some cork with you.'

THREE SINGERS

'What's in a name?' you might ask.

When you're mixed race, a lot hinges on it.

Take Perry Krishna Buckle.

When we met him at the singing class, he introduced himself as PK.

It was not until the third lesson, when we congregated in the pub, that he told my twin sister and me that PK stood for Perry Krishna. His mother was Indian, he said, and she was from Mathura. His middle name was in honour of Mathura, Lord Krishna's birthplace.

My twin Sonali half-shrieked, half-laughed. 'Perry Krishna is a very odd name. But cute, too,' she added.

Then she dug her elbow into me, and announced to him, 'We're quite similar, you know. My middle name is Candida.'

PK looked taken aback. He regarded us closely. He had olive skin, light brown hair, flecked with even lighter wisps and brown eyes. In multi-multi London, he could be from anywhere, any land, any race. Sonali and I had tried to figure out his ethnic antecedents but we never guessed he might be a person with the middle name of Krishna. Of course, we had half-expected that most of the people signing up to classes to sing *thumri* would have some connection to the Indian sub-continent.

That's what you might expect, but in our class of ten, two of whom only showed up once, four are not Asian and they are the ones most deeply interested in all aspects of north Indian light classical music, knowing more about *raag* and the traditions than us. They seem to have studied the music rather than merely enjoyed it. We're here to learn the songs we like to listen to when we are cutting or sewing. We'd put PK in the category of serious hobbyists on a spiritual musical journey; people whom we assumed had no exposure to this kind of music in their home. We learnt to love *ghazals* and *thumri* because our Dad had made us listen to his CDs when we were growing up and given us intense explanations of the singers and the songs.

Everyone in our singing class is pleasant but PK is the only one near our age. We think he's in his late twenties, max early thirties. Although we head to the pub as a group, generally Sonali and I sit closest to him, relishing our chats with him.

That evening after the third lesson PK turned to me after Sonali had announced her middle name. 'What's your name, Himani? Full name, I mean'.

'Himani Charlotte Joy Dalzel Sahni.'

'That's a mouthful. Is your family of Indian origin?' He asked it hesitantly.

Of course, he knew we were. Presumably he could easily guess from my first and last name. What he was asking was, 'Are you mixed race? Really?'

It was obvious he hadn't guessed. Because, again, in London, with our dark hair, dark eyes, our average height and our names, we were firmly South Asian in our appearance. The slight give-away of Sonali's features, different from my own, were detected in India but not here. In one way our Dad was a stereotypical British Asian statistic because he was an ENT consultant. In his early youth he'd had a moustache but that had gone when he decided to settle in London. Our mum was English, from the Lakes. She had studied architecture but didn't practice it. She had brown hair and light blue eyes which neither of us had inherited.

We're non-identical twins. We've always adored each other. We did have the occasional quarrel and it was usually because Sonali, who was older by two whole minutes felt she could boss me about, disapprove of the clothes I wanted to wear, or the subjects I wanted to study, or the boys I wanted to hang out with.

We parted ways at university so we could be free of each other and the people who knew us as twins. We enjoyed that phase of striking out on our own but somehow on our twenty-seventh birthday we agreed that we were most comfortable with each other and that we should work together. Sonali had the design experience and I had the MBA. After a year of toying with the idea we finally set up our own small fashion business. We named our label 'Two Singers'.

*

We loved singing, although we weren't very good at it. I was better at holding a tune, but Sonali opened her mouth more when she sang, as she wasn't shy, and she sang loudly and lustily. When we signed up for the group sessions to learn semi-classical songs, there was an unsaid assumption that we might meet some like-minded men in a neutral but fun environment. It was too bad that we were both currently single and unattached. I reckoned that even if we didn't meet anyone interesting we'd have spent some evenings doing something we loved. The classes were my idea because I don't like my time to be wasted.

Well, we met PK, and hit it off from the first session, but there weren't two of him. Unless...

My response to PK's question was to say that yes, we were Indian, or part-Indian and part-English, or just English, whichever way he liked to cut it; knowing that he would understand like nobody else would. I asked if he had a twin. Or a brother...

'I'm an only child,' he replied.

*

At home Sonali and I guess PK's shoe size and shirt size. We guess what his mother might look like, since he seems to have taken entirely after his father. There are not many traces of Indian-ness in him. We wonder if he feels the same connection to our city, and whether he feels that pull towards Indian culture just because one parent took the time to inculcate an interest. We wonder what's brought him to the singing sessions.

I like him. He has an earnest air about him; he's not an aggressive type, his manners are refined, he's handsome. He's a good listener but he doesn't tell us that much about himself, except when you ask him a leading question. Sonali, on the other hand, drip-feeds him too much information about us, including telling him I'm the 'geeky' one. He looked startled at that, rightly so. I suspect Sonali likes him too, more than she's letting on.

There's a half-term break in our lessons and then we're back in the church hall for our first session after two weeks. We have six more to go. Then we can sign up to another term if we like. Our teacher is trying to gauge interest, as she has to fix the dates with the hall and pay a deposit. I wonder if our voices carry out into the nave of the empty church and if the statues turn their ears towards us. What would the Virgin Mary make of the songs we like to rehearse? *Thumri* lyrics and melodies were written for courtesans, about two hundred years ago, and sung by them to entice and entertain their patrons. The compositions were based on classical *raag* and on devotional folk lyrics, but the words are flirtatious, and about the relationship between lovers. Often we sing about an ache for a missing lover. I can relate to that, I think. It's not that I'm missing anyone in particular, at this moment, it's more that I'm missing having someone to miss. The songs make me weepy inside and I sing them softly.

I don't know what music sounded like when Jesus was a youth but no doubt people all over the world sang or chanted and even two thousand years ago enthusiastic groups must have exercised their lungs together, and that joy hasn't changed.

Sonali pipes up to tell the tutor that we would sign up for the next term. 'We *love* it', she states. 'The classes have definitely met our expectations.'

I wonder if PK will last six more weeks in the course, and then another twelve thereafter. He's certainly been committed to the sessions, but life outside of this may take over. He's often mentioned his past travels. How many Thursday evenings will he give up to this amateur singing group? We are only six regulars now, with two others dropping in when they can. But the six of us, led by our teacher, make a good harmony.

We begin to sing a slow *thumri*. The lyrics of this one are based on Radha's love for Lord Krishna. '*Mora*

Sanyan Mose Bole Na'. I sort-of join in, but as Sonali can be heard 'aaa – aaa – aahing' in a heartfelt but showy manner, I burn with indignation. She has a habit of flirting with the men I like before I can get round to it. Is she now going to make moves on PK without checking with me first?

In the event it is Sonali who is miffed when PK asks me to have a coffee with him.

'How about Saturday afternoon?' he said to me. 'I'm interested in hearing more about your fashion start-up.'

Sonali had gone to the loo when he asked. I broke it to her on the way home.

She was so astonished she actually said out loud what she was thinking. 'I thought he'd prefer me!'

That is what she said. My twin.

She sets my teeth on edge the way she assumes that every male in the universe will think of her as the more attractive one. We both know that it's not true; experience has proven that some men do exist who fancy me more than her. To be sure, in most of our unspoken wranglings over the same boys when we were teenagers, Sonali always felt she had first dibs. But why now, why today, does she believe PK would favour her?

What's so special? Is she preening herself on our differences? Sonali is precisely one inch taller than me. She makes a deal about it. Like she does about her pointy chin, which is like our mother's. She also has our mother's soft eyebrows, small nose and thin mouth. I have more striking brows and fuller lips.

My belly jabs at itself with fingers of acid. PK has individual looks I think, and an independent brain, and he asked me to coffee.

I won't let her upset me. She does say this sort of thing

sometimes, oblivious to how it hurts me. I know we are all navigating the world based on our appearance and other people's gut response to it, but it is crazy that my sister can have the perception of only her own beauty.

'My personality,' Sonali says sharply, suddenly aware of what is going on in my head. 'I thought he would like my style.' She presses her lips into a pained expression, turning herself into the aggrieved party.

To appease her I say that PK wanted to hear more about our work and see our designs.

She snaps at me immediately: 'I'm the designer. Did you tell him that? *I* do all the work.'

I glare at her. 'I'll be sure to tell him on Saturday. I'll tell him that you do all the work. I'll tell him I have the brain. I'll tell him I wrote the business plan. And I can cut and sew too. *And* I have to make the sales pitches with you.'

*

On Saturday, Sonali went for a swim while I met PK. I wasn't really sure that I was on a date. Coffee is not really a 'date date', is it? PK and I have a happy and easy conversation. The fact that we have sung together, when neither of us are cut out to be singers, makes us very relaxed in each other's company. I'm surprised that he actually does ask a lot of questions about our work.

'Was it really your business plan that got you the loan, Himani?' he says. 'I'd like to see it.' He notices my hesitation. 'If you don't mind, of course. You may not want a stranger checking your plan and stealing your secrets. But I may be able to offer some tips.'

'You're not a stranger,' I tell him, feeling flattered that he wants to see the schedule of business growth that I've devised. He told us before that he's an IT consultant but today he's shared the fact that he also has a business background. His father owns a small chain of supermarkets, a franchise of high-end watch dealerships, and real estate, among other things. PK says he usually doesn't like to mention his family business empire.

I am curious about why he's at the *thumri* class but I don't ask him outright.

I babble a bit about my reasons instead. 'Some friends like to learn Bollywood dancing. I mean, not just Asian friends, but everyone. But when it comes to loving Hindi film songs, both old and new, it's only people from South Asia or that heritage, right? Some of our friends think it's weird that we're more interested in light classical music. I keep telling them that the film songs are based on classical *raags*. They don't get our obsession with *thumri* but I think it's something that reminds us of our childhood. Then, we used to sigh that we were being force-fed this additional culture; now we listen to it by choice, especially when we're working.'

PK gives an understanding nod. He discovered *thumri* when he was dragged to concerts in Delhi while he was visiting friends. He had such a wonderful time on that visit that he was trying to re-create some of that magic in London. 'I'm trying to gain more of an insight into the art-form so I can fully appreciate it when I go to a live recital again,' he says, looking endearingly earnest.

I let my heart indulge in little leaps of delight. I want to sit closer, touch his hands, tell him about upcoming concerts at the South Bank, and we could go together.

'I don't even fully understand the words,' he says wistfully. 'At least Sonali and you speak the language.'

'Not very well,' I assure him. 'But yes, of course, we can get by. As for the lyrics, they're not that different from song to song. My mother always says: there's the monsoon, and the lovers are either separated and pining, or about to get together. Even she's an expert.'

I don't mention that he sometimes mispronounces the words we sing in the class. I'm staring at his shoulders, thinking I could have a fusion Indo-Western jacket made for him and how good he would look in it, when he asks, 'Coffee again, Himani? Next Saturday? Same time, same place?'

Another coffee? I think. Another Saturday afternoon? A tame time, I think.

I try not to be too disappointed that he pecks me airily on both cheeks when he goes off. I mean I *am* disappointed but he hasn't led me to expect anything more.

At the Thursday singing lesson Sonali is subdued and I'm grateful for that. She's not muscling in now. He's attracted to me, I think to myself. Me. He likes me for my intellect and poise and self-sufficiency, and my wavy thick hair, all things he's complimented me on. I find myself smiling a lot more at everyone in the class. When I exchange a look with PK I know I shine with happiness.

The next Saturday PK tells me more about himself. He seems quite intent that I get to know his background. He seems to have been lonely at boarding school while being a high-achiever. He doesn't say so, but I'm drawing my own conclusions as he shares some of his memories. His parents are divorced. He asks me my experience of being mixed race. 'Do you feel English? British? Indian? Wholly of one culture? A bit of both? Disconnected from both?'

'Disconnected?' I say, puzzled. 'I think of myself as multifaceted, blessed. I am not A *or* B; I am A+B, I am lucky to draw the best from two cultures.'

I am very emphatic on this point and he quickly nods, although he looks sad.

'You couldn't possibly have a problem, PK, with not fitting in,' I say, 'not with your looks.'

He grins then. 'I don't have a problem; I'm just sometimes confused. Now, has the intelligent multifaceted person brought the business plan?'

I love his cheekbones when he grins like that. I hand him a folder of some pages that I'd photocopied for him. I did want to show off – I couldn't help it.

'If you don't mind, I'll read it right now,' he says. He orders another coffee and studies the document. I begin to wonder then if one reason he prefers my company is that I'm quiet, unlike Sonali. I'm watching his concentration but not showing how restive I'm getting. What kind of relationship does he want? The question races around my brain while I try to tranquilise my disobedient heart.

PK finishes reading and returns the folder to me. 'Do you need an investor?' he asks.

'Why?' is the first response that escapes my lips.

'If you do, I would like to invest in your business.'

My insides sink and soar at the same time. A cash injection would be marvellous. PK, essentially an outsider, showing conviction in our work is even more wonderful. But if he becomes our business partner will he be a boyfriend? Wouldn't that be too complicated? Focus on the positive, I think. We could employ a tailor. We must have won PK's trust if he wants to put money into our venture. He must be sure he'll get a good return. He must be *very* impressed with my business plan.

PK leans forward. 'I feel like you're my sisters.'

I want to crash through the floor.

The Planet Spins On Its Axis, Regardless

Yet I'm still sitting here, hiding my wounds. I am beginning to comprehend him. He's investing in *family*. We've won his affection. But I haven't managed to steal his heart and fly away with it and I won't be bringing it back with the monsoon clouds.

I haven't managed to say a word to him yet. PK raises his coffee mug to his lips, twists his mouth in distaste at the dregs, puts the mug down and smiles. 'Himani Charlotte,' he croons softly, persuasively, lifting a finger. 'Sonali Candida'. Another finger. 'Perry Krishna'. He lifts a third finger. 'A minor re-brand is all that's required,' he says. 'Three Singers'.

WHEN YOU GO
YOU LEAVE A FARCE

I arrive in Ujjalpur when the unbearably bright July sun is at its peak in the sky. The villagers want to know my name. That much is obvious. But they don't have to ask me. By the time I alight at my destination from the car I have hired to bring me here, the driver has already stopped a few times to ask the way to the house of my cousins. A raggle-taggle bunch of youths with nothing better to do have been following the slow-moving car at their own pace.

When the lane narrows down to just a *gali*, when the cows, stray dogs and bicycles-balancing-cans-of-paint all take precedence, the spanking white car can go no further, and the driver stops and points to the black-railed gate a few yards ahead. 'That must be it. The house of your cousins.'

The house is painted a fetching pink. I have four female relatives in this village – well, four who are of my generation – and two of them live in this house. I last saw them when I was twelve years old. One of them is my first cousin and although the other three are close in age to me the actual relationships are complicated. One is my father's cousin, but born around the same time as his daughter. Another is my father's uncle's adopted niece from his wife's side. To simplify things, I refer to them as I have always done, as 'cousins', although as soon as the word 'cousin' is mentioned to friends in India who don't know the family, an explanation of the blood relationship is usually pumped out of me.

When I was younger and I was taken to Ujjalpur more often by my father, us four girls played all day if it was school holidays for them too. We played Seven Stones, Catch, Mother May I, Hopscotch. We played L-o-n-d-o-n, London! Who knew then that Daddy and I would later live permanently in London and hardly ever return to India, let alone Ujjalpur. We played Hide and Seek. My preferred hiding place was the in the darkness of the quilt storeroom, where you could climb aloft a stack of ten thick folded *razai* and nap on the top till you were found.

*

I haven't seen my cousins in the flesh for eighteen years, but as they pour out of the pink house to exclaim over me I realise that mentally I will revert to referring to them as I have always done: Skinny Cousin, Singing Cousin, Stodgy Cousin and Simpering Cousin. Their adult selves are, utterly surprisingly, not that different from their pre-teen selves.

My suitcase and rucksack are carried inside by many willing hands while I submit to intense hugs and murmurs of condolences. We live, therefore we condole. We show we care. This is how things are done. I begin to accept the fact that I will have to repeat some parts of my father's story twenty times a day while I am on this trip. His accidental death, his last wishes. My father, who liked to be orderly in all matters, has specified in a letter attached to his will that his ashes be taken to Ujjalpur and offered to the water. To the river here, specifically. This is puzzling to me but I reason that a branch or two of his family still live here and he must have had an unspoken affection for this village in the Himalayan foothills where he grew up. Whatever the intention, I said aloud to Daddy when I had read the letter twice, to be sure of his wishes, *It has been asked and it shall be done.*

I am introduced to the husbands and children dropping by from the different households of the cousins, and an assortment of elderly cousin-aunts has gathered in the living room. People who knew my father are milling in the courtyard while distant relatives are dotted about in all the cool white rooms. I can see that I'm going to have to be firm about spending my short time here with my four cousins. I'd already explained my mission to them on the phone and at each juncture now I repeat my previous suggestion that I don't need the entire extended clan to come en masse with me for the offering of the ashes to the water. I would like to be accompanied by just the girls I once knew. I know how this is received, but as I'm a misfit anyway, with foreign ways to boot, I can get away with it. They will say behind my back that I'm strange and I don't know how things should be done, I have been away too long, blah blah. I don't care what they say when I'm not there to hear it as long as I don't have to pour out Daddy's ashes with a crowd in tow. There was nothing in his letter about holding a memorial or a prayer ceremony in a temple here. He would have said if that was what he wanted, he knew how to make his views clear.

So one of my recurrent sentences today turns out to be: 'I'm just following instructions.' When I get a moment alone I turn my eyes up to the white ceiling and address it. *You see, Daddy, how dutifully I'm following your directions. I'm here, in the family home in Ujjalpur. I hope you're pleased.* I glow with virtue.

*

Skinny and Simpering live in the pink house with their families. Singing and Stodgy have also stayed in the area and both have contrived to buy homes in a new complex on the perimeter of the village. 'Duplex villas' is how they refer to their terraced houses. I am taken for a tour of their fresh-yellow-painted abodes. In my mind I see a vision of the pink house (old) and the yellow houses (new) side by side, and together like this, in my mind, pink and yellow, pink and yellow, they remind me of wild lantana flowers. How abundant the massed green shrubs were on the roads that led to this village; how I loved to stare at the tiny, profuse pink and yellow florets; how I loved to smell them and pick them apart to create a dainty trail of my wanderings. The lantana has been cleared as a dominating weed, but just thinking about it, the air in Ujjalpur begins to smell like lantana, a sharp herby tang gladdens my nostrils even in this high heat and my fingers itch to fidget with a pink and yellow inflorescence.

In the evening I'm informed by Singing's husband – ex-military, now a businessman ('property deals, this and that, you know') – that it's odd that my father asked for his ashes to be immersed in Ujjalpur. Strictly speaking it's not a river that runs past this village. It's only a stream. 'But,' he concedes, 'it *is* a tributary rivulet of the Ganga. And we're not that far from Haridwar.'

'It's what he wanted,' I say, for the umpteenth time. 'It's equally a mystery to me, but I am here at his request.'

Singing Cousin has arranged a pundit, the best in the village, to help me perform the ceremony. 'Must I drag the priest along,' I ask? 'Can I not go the water's edge and do the deed myself?'

Simpering's face transforms into a mask of horror. I have my answer. If you involve family for their help, then you have to let them meddle a little bit. It is only polite. I let them meddle. I decide to follow their subsequent instructions meekly.

*

We bathe early the next morning and each of us dresses in a white *salwar-kameez*. The pundit arrives at the gates an hour after he said he would. A tempo van, complete with local driver, has been arranged for the six of us by Singing's husband. It is waiting at the end of the lane. We set off to the river. Ten minutes later we park on the last stretch of built road and begin to walk across a swath of pebble and shingle to the river. Across shingle we walk but the river doesn't materialise. It is not there. It appears to have dried up overnight.

'I checked last week and the stream was normal.' Singing looks stunned. 'There was plenty of water.'

'They are damming it further up,' Skinny informs me. 'To clear the silt, I believe'.

'Oh yes, I do remember hearing that there would be some work upriver. The damming must have started.' Simpering spreads her hands at fate. 'But why today?'

Stodgy steps out into the middle of the riverbed where there is a large puddle. The remainder of the riverbed is a damp long line with a few more puddles further ahead in small basins of lower ground. 'Here?' asks Stodgy, looking hopefully at me.

I look at the sky. *This is the spot, Daddy. Now what do I do?*

The Planet Spins On Its Axis, Regardless

When she sees me hesitate, Simpering suggests that I can return when the work upriver has finished and the rivulet has been let loose again.

I want to ask her if she knows the price of an air ticket. I want to ask her if she knows that I get two weeks holiday a year. Am I going to make a trip to Ujjalpur again in a few months? Can I tell her that I prefer to spend my holiday money on a ski trip in the winter?

How mean I'm being, how unfair to my father. He has left me with enough money for fifteen ski trips so I shouldn't begrudge this at all. I'm holding a large plastic container filled with his ashes and small bits of white bone that I hope belong to him, but who knows how they scoop out things in the crematorium, where it's a conveyor belt of one body after another, and a set time to burn. Even dead, you can't take too long or be stealthily quick, you just follow the timetable.

I stand on a dry riverbed of gravel wondering what to do. It strikes me that there may have been a hidden agenda in my father's request. There was no way I'd come to Ujjalpur if he hadn't specifically asked for this. Maybe I'm over-analysing. He may have had a huge nostalgic love for his familial village and I wasn't aware of it. He just wants to rest in peace here. But although he's succeeded in sending me here, and I will leave his ashes here, you can bet that *my* ashes are not coming here. I will send mine via ski-lift to a snow-clad summit, to be thrown over a precipice.

A group of five raggedy children is hovering on the riverbank. Although the riverbed is waterless they don't play on it.

The priest breaks into my silent thought. 'We can perform the ceremony here anyway.'

He spreads a sheet on the pebbles, at a distance from the puddle, removes his greyish Reebok trainers and sits down cross-legged. He is carrying an Adidas bag with pink piping. His white *dhoti* and his beige *kurta* are wonderfully clean and starched. Simpering Cousin obediently sits down beside him, her legs folded beneath her. I remain standing. While I am considering what to do, the others have removed their shoes and sat down and the pundit has taken out his little accoutrements from the bag, and without me, they are beginning the ceremony of last rituals. The pundit chants Sanskrit *shloka* and pours a teaspoon of holy water into the cupped palms of my four cousins which they hold for a second before letting the drops of liquid meet the dry ground.

'Your turn,' says Skinny one.

I sit down and repeat the exercise.

The translucent white plastic jar is taken from my arms. The lid is unscrewed. A small amount of the ashes is duly distributed to cupped palms once again and carried by the four cousins to the middle of the riverbed where they drop the ashes into the puddle. I find I am standing again, standing and thinking furiously, but I follow this exercise too. The pundit arises and walks towards where the rivulet should be, wincing at the sharp jabs of the stones into his soft bare feet. He begins to turn the plastic jar upside down to shake out all the ashes into the puddle. A breeze starts up and blows them towards the children. One of them, a girl with a dirt-streaked but intensely sweet face, comes running up and says, in the nicest, politest way, 'Uncle-ji, when you have finished with this *dabba*, can I have it? Give it to me, Uncle-ji, not the others.' She stands by his side waiting.

I shake myself out of my stupor. 'Stop!' I call out. 'Stop.'

The pundit stops shaking out ashes, holds the large container upright and waits for me to say more.

'Shouldn't there be water?' I ask. 'Isn't that the whole *point* of the ceremony?'

Singing Cousin looks at me. 'Is it? Is that the point?'

Simpering says, 'Well if you can't come back when the river runs...'

And Stodgy stands in front of the pundit, hands on hips, 'Should there be water? More than this?' She points at the sad puddle.

He wavers. He looks at his watch. 'Well,' he begins, 'we have had the ceremony and this is the requested spot... '

I cut in. 'There must be water. There is no cleansing without water.' Although I'm sure my father didn't believe so totally in these religious rituals, depositing him into a puddle doesn't seem right. There is going to have to be a bit more water. Something better than this. I set my lips. I am not known as Stubborn for nothing.

The four cousins are looking at me annoyed. I wrest the container from the pundit and return to the sheet on the ground, which is now pinned down by trainers and sandals neatly placed at the four corners. I pick up the lid and slowly screw it on to the top. As I do this, I hear the pundit say, 'Allotted time is up. It will cost more.'

Skinny nods at him. 'No problem,' she says.

'I suggest,' he says ponderously, 'since your sister from London wants more water, that we go to Madhuban Lake. The lake is always full and it's clean.'

Skinny nods again, approvingly. The others look doubtful. 'There *is* a tradition of letting go of ashes on the lake,' says Skinny.

Pundit, who is gathering up his teaspoons and salvers and little bowls of stainless steel, gives a hum of assent.

I look up at the sky again. *Ujjalpur river is not cooperating, Daddy. This puddle won't do for you. I'm sorry. We're going to have to compromise. We're going to a lake. A lake that's full and clean.*

I nod agreement at the priest.

'For the lake,' he declares, 'we need a small jar. Because it has to go under the water. That is the correct way to offer the ashes if you're going to the lake.' He points to the container cradled to my chest. 'That's not right for setting on the lake.'

'There are hardly any ashes left anyway,' Stodgy says.

He rustles in the Adidas holdall and comes up with a small glass jar, which has *kumkum* red powder in it. The pundit considers for a moment, then he tips out some powder on his palm, places his thumb on it and anoints us all with a red tikka on our forehead. He raises the glass jar but there is still some vermilion in it. He sighs and sprinkles it out on to the gravel. He holds the glass jar out towards me. I understand. Carefully, I put the lip of the plastic to the lip of the glass and shielding the operation with my body I pour out the ashes and the last of the bits of bone from one container into another. The glass is still tinged red with the powder clinging to it and the grey ashes inside have assumed a cheery pink cast. The pundit then covers the neck of the jar with a square piece of muslin, which like a magician he has conjured from the depths of his *kurta* pocket, and he ties it around the neck of the jar with yellow pure-cotton thread.

When he breaks off the thread Simpering Cousin holds out her wrist, and he separates the thick strands so that the remainder of the thread can be tied on to our wrists. We are now spiritually connected to the glass jar of pink ashes by sacred yellow thread. Pink and yellow, I think, pink and yellow for ashes and thread, pink and yellow for lantana flowers, pink and yellow for all my jumbled memories of Ujjalpur.

The raggedy girl comes and stands by me, her eyes on the container in my hands. I place it on the ground and not a beat passes before she picks it up and runs away with it. I hope it's for her mother; for grain, or lentils. The other kids chase her.

'I didn't know there was a lake here too,' is my conversation offering, as our group of five women aged thirty to thirty-eight, and one emollient priest, aged what? – forty to forty-five? – heads back to the hired tempo.

'It's only a small lake,' says Singing Cousin.

'And it's not in Ujjalpur, technically,' adds Simpering. 'It's a forty-minute drive!'

'I've never been there,' says Stodgy.

This makes the others giggle. Stodgy looks irritated.

We arrive at Madhuban Lake. I am the first out of the tempo to see if there is water. I exhale in relief. There is water, plenty of it, gleaming in the noon sun. The lake is not that small, it ripples gently into the distance. Although I can see the shore on the other side, because the lake is not very wide, I can't see the perimeter of the lake to my right. The water stretches away in a narrow strip to the horizon, enclosed by green trees. Quite like a river, in fact. I begin to feel better.

Two boatmen approach us. We state our business. One of the boatmen elbows aside the other and stands forward. 'It's me you want,' he says. 'That's my business. Sending off the ashes.'

Simpering asks, 'Why you?'

'Because I'm the one who does it. He doesn't.'

He's lying, of course, but the other doesn't argue, he looks fatigued. Maybe noon is not his best time. Our self-appointed boatman bustles about, wading into the water to bring round his boat and to instruct us to roll up our *salwars*. Stodgy looks faint. The rest of us take a few steps into knee-deep water where the boatman helps us into the boat and tells us where to sit on the two benches. Pundit on the left, Simpering on the right. Skinny on the left. 'You here, *behenji*,' says Boatman, settling me on the right, and 'You sit here, sister, in the middle, he says to Singing. Stodgy is still standing at the water's edge, a distinct look of unease on her face.

'She's scared of water,' murmurs Singing.

'Then she should stay on land,' decides the boatman.

Stodgy hears him and is incensed. 'Did you hear why we are here?' she shouts across to him. 'My uncle's ashes', she says dramatically. 'Do you think I would not get on the boat?'

The boatman looks at Singing, looks heavenward, shrugs.

We wait. Five minutes pass. Singing is humming a muted *bhajan*, Simpering is ensuring her fair hands are covered by her *dupatta* and I'm shading my eyes to take in the beautiful scenery. Why haven't I been to this serene spot on earth before? Daddy will like it here; anyone would.

Stodgy has put one foot in the water. It is on the tip of my tongue to urge her on. But I know she has many phobias and I don't want to be responsible for killing her. Fear might kill her.

The Planet Spins On Its Axis, Regardless

I look at the boatman whose impatience has made his face red, but he stays silent. It is not his place to say anything. On a signal from the pundit, he loosens the mooring rope and the boat drifts out into the water. Stodgy is stunned into action; she is at the side of the boat in great splashes. The boatman and the pundit haul her in. She is hyperventilating. The boatman manoeuvres her to the middle of the first bench. He takes his position at the back of the boat, stows the rope, puts his hands on the oars, and addresses Stodgy: 'Don't worry auntie, if you just sit still we will all be completely safe...'

'What did you say?' Stodgy glares at him and shifts again causing a rocking of the vessel.

'I said not to worry auntie, I'm an experienced boatman.'

'Why are you calling me auntie?' she roars. 'Do I look like an auntie to you?'

The boatman gapes at her.

'I'm the youngest of this lot,' she says. 'Don't call me auntie. I'm not your auntie. Understand?'

'I understand.' Boatman is cowed and rows furiously till we are centred between the two shores. Singing, Simpering and Skinny can't control their smirks. Pundit keeps a straight face. Stodgy is still trembling with fear. I'm clutching the jar with the tinted ashes. The water gleams, the fronds of trees dipping in at the shores are the colour of old Kashmiri jade and the sun is relentless in its radiant beauty. I'm ready to let go of the ashes.

'What do I do?' I ask Pundit when Boatman stops rowing and lets the boat drift.

'Leave the jar on the water.'

'But the ceremony...' interrupts Singing. 'The ritual, the ceremony?'

Pundit obliges. He begins chanting a *shloka*, at least that's what I assume he's reciting. What do I know? He looks very solemn as he slows the chant down to elongated vowels. I am waiting for him to say, '*Om Shanti Shanti*', words I *do* know. I follow the four cousins in folding my hands and looking down in earnest prayer. A mobile phone rings. We look up startled. Pundit stops intoning, delves into his starched *kurta* pocket and answers his phone. Into the instrument he says, 'Yes. No. Not now, later. Soon. I'll tell you what time, I'll try to bring it. I can't talk, I'm working. I can't talk now, I just told you, I'm in the middle of work.' He puts away his phone and resumes the chant. There is no apology. The interruption is not mentioned either by Pundit or by the four cousins who are as saucer-eyed as I am. If Boatman thinks anything at all he is not showing it.

I place the jar on blinding sunlight in the water. It bobs away towards the far end of the lake. We all stare after it. I didn't realise the wind was rippling the water to such a degree. Our boat had felt like it was drifting rather slowly, but I guess the boatman's oars were holding us in place. I see a bird alight on the jar. Its claws grip the cloth tied around the neck. It pecks its beak into the soft muslin.

'What will happen now?' I ask. Aren't the ashes meant to go in the water? The jar will bob out of sight before I can see what will happen to it. Will the birds pick it up and take it away? I see another one alight on it. 'What do those horrible crows want?' I ask.

Pundit doesn't answer but Boatman does. 'The birds want cloth for their nests. They will peck at the jar and their weight sitting on it will soon send the jar under. Don't worry,' Boatman reassures me, 'your father's ashes will go in the water, in this beautiful place, just as he wanted.'

I like Boatman better than Pundit.

I turn my head away from the others. *It's a nice day, Daddy, clear strong sunshine, sparkly water, lashings of green fronds. If you ignore the people here, everything is perfect, and you are in Nature's bosom. I won't tell you to have a lovely time swirling in Madhuban Lake. I know what was important. You knew how to have a wonderful time when you wished.*

TULIP PERSIMMON'S HEAD-WETTING

Gilt cherubs gazed down from the pale blue ceiling. Holding their dainty lyres like shields they watched Karina, stumbling creature that she was, make her entrance into the thronged ballroom. She looked up at the cherubs, murmured a hello to them, took another step forward and found that she was in a line for something. She tuned in to the conversation around her. It was the queue to sign the guest book. She worried her nail tip as she waited. Her friends, Rahul and Gavin, should have said on the invitation that everyone would be asked to write a commemorative line or two for baby Tulip. She would have come prepared.

As she neared the table she saw that it wasn't a book at all, but a long scroll of cream parchment patterned with tulips. She guessed these were hand-drawn by one of the proud dads, probably Rahul. Gavin and he were both artistic but Rahul was the better painter. The curly-haired woman ahead of her straightened up and handed her a fountain pen engraved with cobalt and gold tulips. Karina, admirer of beautiful objects, twirled the pen in her fingers, examining it and wondering at the cost of it. Perhaps the pen had been especially commissioned by Gavin.

Aware of an impatient rustle behind her she turned her attention to the scroll. The golden nib of the pen met the parchment and offered it a dot, a splodge created by her hesitation. She lifted the nib and read a few of the inscriptions. The other invitees had jotted down smart and witty aphorisms for Tulip. Where had they found these sayings? Off the top of their heads? She felt the closeness of the person behind her, the shift into her space, and precipitously, she gave up, handing the fountain pen to the man behind her with an apologetic, 'I need to think of something to say.' She walked away from the embarrassment of her unexplained dot on the parchment.

Wading through the long legs and sharply dressed elbows of the crowd she got to a spike-haired waiter from whose tray she picked up a flute of pink champagne. More at ease with a glass in her hand she stood by the wall and scanned the room. High-ceilinged, cavernous and painted duck-egg blue. This building had been a duchess's home in the late eighteenth century. Restored to neo-classical opulence it now billed itself as London's most glamorous private club. White clouds bordered by gold floated on the blue ceiling above her. Those cavorting naked cherubs watched her, judging her navy pencil skirt with its red trim, and her navy velvet jacket. They could see into her useless empty uterus.

Karina's darting black eyes had not caught sight of a baby yet. Where was the guest of honour, the reason for the party? She spotted Gavin and Rahul in the centre of the room under the crystal droplet chandelier, being embraced by the beautiful multitudes, but she was apprehensive they'd ask her what she'd inscribed for baby Tulip. Rahul would ask if she'd written something in Hindi as well. She must first sign the scroll before she went up to give them her own congratulatory hugs.

She rifled through her head for snatches of poems, quotations, wisdom. Something that would be memorable for Tulip Persimmon Dutta-McDougall. Something the girl would like to read later on. When Karina was thirteen, there had been a fashion for autograph books in her school in Delhi. All the girls had bought one and they'd passed it around the class for their friends to sign. Karina was the only one actually leaving her class that year. Her father had been transferred to the consulate in London and he'd promptly arranged for her to board at a school in Gloucestershire where she could finish her schooling regardless of his further transfers. In the first few months in England she'd missed her friends and looked often at her autograph book. She knew by heart what everyone had written, the silly rhymes, the sincere I-will-miss-you scrawls.

The boy she had liked best, the one she would love forever in her frozen memory of his boy-state, wrote: 'Have a good life.' As bald as that. She would never see him again. Nothing had spoiled the memory of her crush, not even his limp autograph. Maybe he'd grown up to be ruthless, slightly paunchy and a trifle smug, like her boss. He might have become someone she would barely tolerate, if she met him now. Or maybe he'd become a computer genius, nerdy or marginally bohemian, absorbed into Silicon Valley. No matter. It didn't concern her if he himself was having a good life or not. It was the boy-he-had-been that she loved forever.

She remembered another autograph from her book, a little rhyme painstakingly written out in elongated flourishes. It was signed by someone she'd not really noticed or spoken to in her school years. The boy was two years above, if she remembered right. She certainly hadn't asked him for a memory, but he'd somehow gotten hold of her book and written:

The grass is green/ The rose is red/ I will love you/ Till I am dead.

So far nothing appropriate for Tulip Persimmon. Karina kept the brain pages turning. Surely another glass of pink champagne, another smile from the handsome waiter would help? Yes. A poem perhaps. *What is this life if, full of care/ We have no time to stand and...* no, no, not appropriate. Why had she regressed to thirteen years old this evening? She should act her age; be the mature thirty-eight-year-old that she was.

*

'Hello, you realise you're talking to yourself – you look quite funny.'

Sahil, her husband. They pressed their lips to each other's chastely. She raised her glass. 'My fave.'

'Hmm... good. What were you babbling to yourself about? You look crazy.'

Her withering look had no effect. 'Did you see the guest scroll we've got to sign?'

At his nod, she said, 'Fantastic idea, but I can't think what to write. Why don't you sign it for us?'

No doubt he'd bypassed it as something she would do or had done. He would have started socialising already. Sahil never dithered.

'Oh no. Not me.'

'Why not?'

'Because if I do, I'll just write something banal, then you'll go over to read it, then you'll come up to me and say it's barely legible and lacks sincerity and I should've at least given it some thought and then we'll have a row.' He picked up a glass from spike-head's tray and released a 'mmmm' when he had sipped the extraordinarily buttery champagne.

'Are we having a row now?' Karina mumbled, 'because you've refused to sign the scroll on our behalf?' She was talking to herself because it didn't seem like he'd heard.

'You wouldn't think they could have it all,' he lifted his chin at the room. 'Rahul and Gavin.'

'I'm not sure they do…. '

'But look at them. A baby now. A girl baby. Is that even allowed?'

Karina knew his words came out of a pit of bitterness. She was just about keeping her own jealousy pressed within. Any moment it would bubble out and a river of slick green saliva would run from her to Rahul and to Tulip, wherever she was, and Karina would be marked out as the wicked witch with ash in her soul.

She wanted to be the good fairy. She wanted to feel happy for Rahul and Gavin. For her and her husband to seem delighted. She wanted to try, at least.

'Sahil,' she said, 'They didn't choose the sex of the baby. As far as I know. I'm not sure you can. Or not in any fool proof way.'

'But that's what they wanted. That's what they have.'

She was silent. It's what Sahil and she didn't have, despite years of trying and two cycles of demeaning treatment.

'Is Ferny here?' Sahil asked. Ferny was Tulip's birth mother.

'No, I don't think she's a part of tonight's jamboree.' Karina waved her hand at the well-dressed people around her. 'I think this is for the parents, the daddies. Look at their faces... how... ' she stopped herself. Talking about the dads' faces was unlikely to make Sahil gleam.

'I've seen the daddies' faces,' he cut in. 'Yes, they're over the moon. I'm sure they will be wonderful parents. Tulip is a lucky girl. But... ' He frowned and his patrician nose indicated disapproval. 'Not everyone is Gavin, not everyone is Rahul. I wonder if this should be allowed?'

'It *is* 2002,' she said brightly, meaning anything could happen now that they were in the twenty-first century and all social conventions could be explained or overturned by dint of living in a new age. It was the reasoning she deployed when she didn't want a discussion to progress. She had her own opinion about Tulip but hadn't formulated a defendable argument and she wouldn't enter the fray unless she was going to win. She returned to an earlier comment Sahil had made. 'I don't think Rahul has it all.' She sneaked a look into her husband's eyes. 'His family won't speak to him or acknowledge him. They won't be mentioning *this* to anyone... '

'Huh... parents. Who cares? Look at him, he doesn't care.'

'*I* know he does. He just won't say so in front of Gavin.'

'Parents are a bother... haven't you noticed?' Sahil put on his jokey voice.

Yes, they'd had plenty of pressure put on them, and misunderstandings about their childless state.

'He's better off not caring.' Sahil's eyes wandered away from her and over her head. He was ticking off the people he knew in the room.

Karina looked across at Rahul, resplendent and perspiring under the central chandelier. Like her, Rahul was from Delhi and when they'd met at university they had bonded over early childhood memories that were similar. She knew that Rahul ached to be accepted by his family. He had told his parents a few times that he was not interested in women. They had ignored him and not enquired further. They preferred denial. Karina had met his parents once. After that she'd tried to dissuade Rahul from sharing too much of his life with them. She knew he would not be able to change their prejudices. It was better for him to accept that some people were beyond changing, they just couldn't do it. It was too much for them. But Rahul had charged recklessly into their precious peace and announced that he was going to live with his partner, had said that he was one-half of a man couple, and that they were going to have a baby. She was not surprised at the reaction from his parents.

Rahul must have sensed her scrutiny because he came towards them and enveloped them in an immense hug. 'What misery am I saving you from?'

'Arguing the demerits of parents,' Sahil replied promptly.

Rahul's eyes clouded but he continued to hold them in his embrace. They voiced their congratulations on the birth of baby Tulip, Sahil managing to sound almost as thrilled as his wife. Karina received a tender squeeze from Rahul in return for her profuse felicitations and she felt emboldened enough to ask if Baby Tulip was attending her head-wetting celebration.

'We don't want her disturbed too much,' Rahul whispered in her ear. 'You know, not too many people breathing on her, or smoking around her. She's in the small drawing room next door, with a nanny. Tell Samantha I sent you to give Tulip a kiss. Knock on the door and say the password, Heavenly Cloud, to be let in.' He squeezed her arm again. 'Only my bestest are being given the password so don't tell anybody else.'

Karina slipped away feeling specially awarded. Sahil would be fine on his own, networking. He would find mutual acquaintances to gossip with. Everyone would be gossiping.

*

'Heavenly Cloud.' She knocked and giggled at the ornate door to the private drawing room. A youthful girl opened the door and giggled back at her, letting her in, and quickly latching the door. Tulip Persimmon was asleep in her baby-carriage. Her long thick lashes lay curled on her cheeks. Her tiny left hand lay on her lips with two fingers wrinkled. They must have just slipped out of her mouth. She was completely undisturbed by the hubbub coming through the door. Karina moved a chair close to the pram and carefully held Tulip's right hand in her palm. 'She's so... small', she whispered to Samantha, 'such a little person.'

Samantha nodded. 'She's just six weeks old.'

'She's adorable.' A tightness in Karina's chest.

Samantha gave another quiet nod.

'Her lashes,' Karina burbled. 'They're like Rahul's. Are her eyes like Rahul's? Sorry, I don't know if you see Tulip regularly,' she added hastily. 'Are you her nanny?'

'Yes. But at the moment both of them are around constantly. I'll spend more time with her when they start up a regular schedule again.' She smiled. 'Little Tulip does have the most fantastic lashes. Wicked.'

'Are her eyes like Rahul's?'

Samantha looked uncomfortable. 'Could be,' she replied. 'It's hard to be sure. Babies change all the time. Some people say she has Gavin's mouth and jaw. We'll have to see when she's a bit older.'

She'd been well trained. She hadn't mentioned Ferny. It was impossible that Tulip had genes from both dads. If they knew who her biological father was, which they must do, they weren't saying. Karina caressed the sleeping baby's right hand for a few minutes, idly noticing that Tulip was not a pink and white baby but olive-skinned. But then Ferny, her mother, was also mixed race. Was that a deliberate choice?

No one put these questions to Rahul and Gavin. It would be too intrusive. She herself knew all about unpleasant invasive questions. Whenever IVF was mentioned. If she raised it herself she didn't mind talking about it in detail. Other times, she couldn't say a word without thinking that she'd snap. Those were the low days. On the more normal days, she sometimes thought that it didn't matter so much, what she had and didn't have; what people asked her or didn't ask her; what they thought her choices were; what advice they doled out unbidden: eat more chillies, learn belly-dancing, get a dog. More difficult to negotiate, more sorrowful, was the chasm that lay between her and Sahil. He seemed not to know when Karina was having an overly-sensitive day. And she wasn't any better with him. They were the absolute worst at reading each other.

She must not sob in front of Samantha. She bent to give Tulip the promised light kiss on her cheek and tried to smile a serene goodbye.

*

The Planet Spins On Its Axis, Regardless

On returning to the ballroom she was offered a cupcake iced with a red tulip from a laden tray. She snuffled it in two bites and slunk along the walls, towards the right of the room, feeling she ought to circulate and also make her way to Gavin, whom she hadn't congratulated yet. She brushed cupcake crumbs off her skirt. The air was thick with voices, laughter, whispers, clinking glasses and wisps of smoke. The gilt cherubs frolicking above now seemed sedate in comparison. This club was no place for a baby. Rahul must have smuggled Tulip in, or got special permission. Were babies allowed in here? She didn't know, but she found herself grinning. Now she was talking like her husband: Is this allowed? Is that allowed?

Who cared?

As she slipped along the periphery, honing her expression of enchantment, she came across a booth screened by black velvet curtains. The heavy drapes were strung on two sets of circular rods, one inner and one outer. A narrow French table stood outside the booth. A delicate white card: Tarot Readings. Karina paused. Was this the amazing reader Gavin often mentioned? The one who got to the heart of the matter and whose wisdom he trusted. Rahul had told her that they both took the guidance of the tarot reader seriously.

She peeked around the first half-drawn curtain. Inside in the shadowy light, she saw a table and two chairs, one of which was occupied by a woman whose pale hair was enhanced by the grey gloom. Cards were stacked in neat decks in front of her. A white hand lifted up, almost ghostly, gesturing for Karina to come in and take a seat. She stared at the fortune-teller, who was preternaturally pale, white-lashed, with colourless lips and wearing a white cotton blouse. It would be rude to walk on now. Timidly, she sat on the vacant chair.

The woman stood up to close the curtains fully, the rings juddering along the rail. Her trousers were black and narrow. She returned to the table and lit the tea lights in their glass jars. A silver bracelet with tiny green charms graced her left wrist. Flames from the candles warmed the dim space making the reader look more other-worldly than she had before.

Karina waited. The two of them eyed each other appraisingly. The tarot reader put out her hand. It was cool to touch. 'I'm Michelle.'

Goodness, she had the honeyed voice of an *apsara*. 'Hi, I'm Karina.'

Michelle said nothing, so Karina asked, 'Have you been busy this evening, lots of people stopping by?'

'Some. I'm a bit hidden in this corner. It's a huge room, and with all those people crushed in the middle, not everyone can see what's at this end.'

'I guess. So... '

'So... '

'Are you going to start?'

'What is your question about?'

'Uh... I don't have a question.'

A patient smile from Michelle. 'It's best to ask a particular question. That is the only way to get a relevant answer.'

Her solemn pronouncement made Karina anxious. This isn't just playing, she thought.

Her question formed as Michelle held up her palm. 'Don't tell me your question yet. Just let me know is it to do with work, family, health, what sort of thing?'

'Uh... family.' Karina looked down. *Will I ever... ?*

Michelle selected a deck of cards and moved the others away. 'Hold this for a minute. Shuffle it please. Now, cut the deck and hand it back to me.' She began to lay out the cards in elegant undulations. 'Before I do the reading, I'd like to ask... how straight do you want it? The truth or just a hedging around?'

Karina considered. But again, before she could answer, Michelle said, 'My readings don't always please people. But I get the feeling you don't want bullshit.'

'No. Tell it like it is, Madame Zelda!'

The tolerant smile that said she'd heard it all before. 'What was your question?'

Karina bit it out. Michelle squeezed up her eyes to view the cards she drew, in the way contact-lens wearers did. Her silky voice began the reading, pointing card by card, as Karina gazed at her fortune splayed on the table.

*

Eventually, the velvet curtains were drawn back to allow her out. She walked on shaky legs, not caring where she was heading, her mind awhirl. She blamed Michelle for her unsteady state, she should complain to Rahul, to someone, anyone, really she should. But she was caught up in a group now, she'd inadvertently lurched towards people she knew, to a corner where her friends were hanging out. She wasn't tall enough to have spotted them across the room before. They were deep in Tulip gossip, but for Karina the choruses ebbed and flowed as if from a distance, and occasionally the word 'baby' crashed around her ears. She couldn't concentrate. No babies. Not for her anyway, according to Michelle. It wouldn't happen. And Sahil didn't want to adopt, Karina knew that. She was going to be left childless. Was it even allowed that a tarot-reader could tell her that?

But the mellifluous Michelle had got extremely animated at the very last card, 'The Lovers', and said that Sahil and she would develop an ideal partnership, fulfilling other ambitions and even being envied because they would have less to fret about than their peers.

According to Michelle, or according to the cards, whichever was the real soothsayer, Sahil loved her deeply, despite not showing it, despite the quarrels about fertility treatments versus adoption versus no children. That last card was a very good omen. It meant that on reflection Karina would work out that it was all for the best. Sahil and she would be a strong team.

The voice had remained musical. Had Michelle noticed how Karina's dark eyes had stayed fixed on the cards in the second row after her interpretation? She had not moved a muscle although cards had continued to be laid down and the voice had carried on its rapid interpretations. Karina's eyes had flickered only at Michelle's dramatic inhalation on the final card.

Perhaps the tarot-reader knew what she was doing. She'd tried to soften the blow. But there was such a thing as hurt ovaries. It wasn't something you could explain. An ache had started low and was spreading up and out like a tree calling for branches. It buzzed into her ears and mouth as she stood there ensconced within her group of friends, unable to heed anything. It will take days to calm myself, she thought, days before I can hear properly, speak sensibly again.

She excused herself from the group to steal along the duck-egg-blue walls, inching back to the guest scroll, which was fatly rolled at the top now with the last of the blank space spread across the table.

Karina picked up the extravagant pen and wrote in a trembling hand: 'Dear Tulip Persimmon, may your daddies always give you as much joy as you have brought to them.'

She stood by the doorway gazing into the room until Sahil's head turned towards her. He was trying to decipher her mood. She messaged him with an eyebrow. She wanted to go home.

He messaged back with a nod, raising his forefinger in a 'give me a minute' sign. She slumped in the doorway. He would be a few minutes.

The buzzing in her head began to die down. The buzzing was tinged with relief. She could just begin to admit it. The not-knowing was over.

Karina straightened up and then slumped again, overcome with remorse at her own behaviour. Unforgivable, she told herself.

*

She had reacted badly in the black velvet cocoon. Fury had got the better of her. She'd wanted to halt that melodious voice, stop it short in the midst of some reassuring phrase, wipe off the patronisingly patient expression, blow out the bloody tea lights, set fire to the halo of white hair.

She'd picked up the cards in the second row that spelt out her answer and torn them. One by one, each card ripped neatly into four pieces. She had hissed at Michelle as she left, 'Thanks, colourless person.'

WHERE HE LIVES

I see him off at the front door. 'I'll try and meet you for lunch,' he whispers. 'Let me get into work, check what I have to deal with and I'll call to fix a time.'

I giggle. We feel like conspirators. Eight months married.

'But, Sabina,' Riyaz's tone is serious, 'go in now and eat a good breakfast. Don't play this game with me.'

So he'd noticed. This morning I'd let his mother set down his *bhurji* and *parantha* and watched like a good wife as he ate it. I was always hungrier than him in the morning, well, all the time, but my mother-in-law's repeated instructions had got to me. She hovered at mealtimes, over the cooker and over her son. She waved away her own comfort. Even when I'd tried, when I'd said, 'You sit down, Ammi-ji, and let me make breakfast for both of you,' she'd shaken her head. It was her kitchen and she knew what her son liked to eat. And pfft, I was so slow. A domestically untrained girl. She reminded me of my ineptitude daily. 'What use is philosophy, Sabina, when one has religion and tradition?' she asked. 'Philosophy is for people with leisure, with nothing to do in their lives.'

*

When I told my philosophy professor at the women's college, Mrs Palli, that I was engaged to Riyaz, she expressed displeasure. At the time I thought her discourteous. Wounding.

'Getting married,' she'd repeated with a sneer. 'You don't want to wait for a few years? Weren't you considering a PhD?'

'It doesn't interest me, ma'am.'

'But going to live in the old city with your boyfriend, that interests you, huh? You'll have to live by the rules of the old city, you know that?'

'He'll be my husband then, ma'am.'

'You may love him but perhaps you're sacrificing your future for him.'

'He *is* my future.' She had no right to interfere.

Mrs Palli flapped her knotty fingers. 'You can wait a few years. You're young.'

'I'm already twenty-four.'

'You'll have to wear a *burqa* and *niqab* every time you step out. If Riyaz loves you, why doesn't he move to the new city?'

'His mother has been in that house for thirty-five years. She won't leave. I don't mind, ma'am, and that's what I told him. We'll be together every day, not meeting in secret, not hiding from the world.' It was all I wanted but I couldn't tell her that.

Her finger tapped the back of my hand. 'You don't understand what you're doing. They live differently in the old city. Women don't have any of the freedoms that you're used to. Do you realise how you'll be expected to dress and behave?'

'I am aware, ma'am.'

'I'm disappointed in you, Sabina.'

I hadn't expected that. The hurt must've shown in my eyes. I bowed my head, tears pricking. 'I'm disappointed in myself too,' I mumbled.

Why had I said that? Her apprehension and her lack of congratulations at my engagement had made me blurt that out. For a moment she'd made me feel desolate and uncertain about the clear-sighted decision I'd made.

I straightened my shoulders. I didn't need her approval even if I admired her. I loved Riyaz. Mrs Palli wouldn't understand. She wasn't young.

Her hands fluttered on my shoulder, as if she was brushing loose threads off a man's jacket. 'Forget what I said.' Her voice turned loud and angry. 'Forget it!' Then in a gentler tone, 'Good luck Sabina. Yes, yes, good luck.'

'Thank you ma'am.'

'Just one piece of advice if I may presume?' She didn't wait for permission. 'Riyaz is a fine young man. Enjoy your first few years together. Don't rush into having a child... '

*

My mother-in-law is a joyless creature. It's an unkind thing to say but is the truth always kind? *People need the truth about their world in order to thrive.* I used that sentence in an essay once. I got top marks. I used to be proud of that.

My mother-in-law likes me to stay home most of the day and do what she does. I help her in her chores. When she sits down with her coffee and listens to the local radio talk show or watches BBC World News on the television, I do the same. I know this is what is expected of me and I do it willingly, but I also need to get out of the house for a walk and to talk to my friends on my mobile. I need to be where she can't hear me. My mother-in-law doesn't like to see people having fun. It's vulgar. Next door to us lives a widow with a raucous laugh. Whenever I hear it, I long to find out what the joke is. My mother-in-law can't stand the woman's laughter. 'A widow,' she remarks, looking pained. 'Laughing so loud we can hear it on our terrace. No shame at all.' My mother-in-law is a widow too, a long-term widow. She wants next door to mooch about all day with downturned lips. 'Life isn't all fun,' she said to me one day. I think I know that. We all know that. That's why fun is important.

She likes me to sit with her at breakfast and lunch. Over breakfast she deliberates on what we will cook for lunch, just us two, and at lunch I get a monologue on what we will cook for dinner. What does darling son Riyaz long for? It wouldn't go down well to tell her that Riyaz longs for me and hardly cares what he eats. I'm the one more interested in food. Food is nutrition for body, mind, soul. As Virginia Woolf said, 'One cannot think well, love well, sleep well, if one has not dined well.'

Riyaz laughed when I quoted this to him. 'Love well,' he echoed. 'Make sure, *begum*, that I have the right food to love well.'

*

Sometimes I do escape in the early afternoon. Riyaz comes to the bazaar in his lunch break and I meet him there. Some days I'm happy and satisfied as we share snacks from the pushcarts. Other days I'm full of resentment and I punish him by going hungry. I see how his cheeks tighten and his lips close in held-in sorrow when I say I don't want to eat. I'm fed up. He understands.

Today when I see him, I'll declare: 'Let's go away for a holiday! For our anniversary. Goa!'

A beach. Just us. Floaty clothes. Prawn curry. Imagine. It won't happen, I know. Not yet. Riyaz has to save money and he won't abandon his mother to waltz off with his wife. I'm working on her so that one day she will suggest it herself: 'Son, why don't you go on vacation to Goa?'

*

The phone rings. My mother-in-law hands it to me with faint disapproval. It's Mrs Palli. Her second call this week. She asks politely after Riyaz.

'He's doing great.'

Last time she asked me if I felt settled.

'Yes,' I'd replied. I knew I sounded sullen.

'Good, good.' Her confident cheeriness. 'If you're settled but not fully occupied, you should come back to study for your PhD. We're assessing applications soon.' A pause. 'You know my hopes for you, Sabina. You were my best student.'

I listen to her intensity today. 'The application deadline is next week. Have you considered it further?'

She wants to mould me into the next Mrs Palli. It was not what I wanted when Riyaz was top of my list, when I was sure I could adapt to anything, anything at all.

I look up at my mother-in-law who has stayed in the room and turned down the volume on the radio. She wants to mould me too. Who am I? What did I agree to be? Riyaz loved me for my exuberance and liberal mind, but now even he suggests that I could behave in a more reserved manner when I'm outside the home as better becomes a woman in a black mantle.

*

My mobile phone pings. It's Riyaz. 'Meet now at Bangle Bazaar crossroads. Sorry, got a bit late. Not much time before I have to get back.'

I half-run to the crossroads. When Riyaz finds me, I take hold of his chin in playful anger. I'm tugging hard at his short beard when a tourist with a big Nikon camera takes a picture of us. It's not the first time. I'm a slim woman in a silky black burqa and niqab, only my eyes visible, and I'm being un-demure. I look at Riyaz. He shrugs. We turn our backs on the tourist and his camera. Riyaz doesn't want confrontation. He never does. Even though the vendors in the market find the constant clicking tiresome, they never step in to admonish tourists either. They need all the business they can get. The outskirts of the new city, where the technology parks are, have become the draw with newly-opened malls and boutiques. Why come to the lanes of the old city unless you live here, have business or family connections here, or are a tourist? As Mrs Palli had cautioned me, no woman goes out uncovered. If tourists take photos, we ignore the intrusion.

Riyaz steers me by the arm to the bakery-café of his school friend, Faroukh. We hover at the entrance. It's packed in there, all the benches heaving. Faroukh clears a space for a foreigner wearing a floppy sun hat. He commands a row of teenage boys to move, and they slide onto another bench, six of them hunched in a space for three. The single female tourist takes the vacated bench. Faroukh has put on his English voice. 'Don't mind the ambience,' he waves his hand at the café, 'but try our home-made snacks. You'll love them. Vegetable puff for you?'

'But I love the ambience,' she protests.

At my side, Riyaz starts laughing. I know he's going to tease Faroukh who's now calling into the kitchen: 'One sugarless tea for the lady.'

He ambles over to us and speaks in his normal voice. 'Two days late,' he complains to Riyaz. 'You were meant to deliver the videos last week. And have tea with me.'

'There's been no time.' Riyaz hands over a USB stick. His colleague at work has been making marketing videos for Faroukh. 'Can't stop today,' he mutters. 'But, soon. I'll come for tea in a day or so.'

'There's no time here either.' Faroukh fills a plate with five different cookies. All are specialties of the house, baked on the premises. He deposits the plate at the tourist's table. Using his English accent again, he lists the flavours and tells her to try them all. She demurs. 'I'll leave the plate here. Try whatever you fancy,' he says, 'and I'll charge you just for what you consume.'

All heads have swivelled towards her but she seems unbothered. She's the only woman sitting in the café. She takes pictures on her phone, first of her little cup of tea, then the plate of biscuits, then surreptitiously she tries to capture Faroukh.

This bakery has been here for sixty years. Faroukh is the fourth-generation owner. When he finished school, he went to the UK for his degree in economics. At least, I think that's what he studied. All good Indian kids who own businesses need to study economics, right? The café lies in the shadow of two ancient mosques. There is not much Faroukh can change in this old space, not that he wants to. Even his dress is the same as his ancestors, worn with more of a flourish. He wears his thick white *kurta* longer than the norm. His white pyjamas stop at ankle length and the plain-looking wide-strapped black sandals on his feet are a designer brand. His white *topi* was crocheted by his grandmother and is a work of art.

He returns bearing a paper packet that he gives to Riyaz. 'Coconut cookies for Sabina. I know they're her favourite.' Riyaz passes the package to me. There's already a sheen of grease on the paper. I wrap two tissues around the packet and slip it into my purse.

'I can see you're busy,' Riyaz says, meaning *I'm* busy. Later he'll tease Faroukh about his self-deprecating conversation with the tourist, not now in front of me and the crowd at the door.

Faroukh is already back at the foreign lady's table, entreating her in his English accent to leave a review on Trip Advisor. He has a series of amazing reviews on there. She is charmed by him. I glance swiftly at her clothes. She's one of those sensible ones, a loose long-sleeved shirt, linen culottes. If she'd come in here in a skirt, she'd have had everyone staring at her legs, except Faroukh of course. Even Riyaz, who is used to women in skirts in his office, and was used to me wearing skirts, albeit long ones, when occasionally he took me out for lunch when we dated, would gaze more than he should if he saw a bare-legged woman in the old city. Context is everything.

'Be appropriate,' my mother always says. *I'm listening*, I tell her silently. Look at me. I'm about to ask Riyaz if he found the lady in the café attractive when a woman clicks by on her powder-blue heels. 'That's Marlie Auntie!' I exclaim, before he can speak.

'You're getting good at this,' Riyaz grins at me with pride.

When I first moved here, we had a ritual. I'd have to guess who the ladies around us in the market or the streets were. Everyone in a *burqa* and *niqab*.

'How do *you* recognise everyone?' I'd ask him.

'Not everyone. But most ladies, yes. See, that one. She has a long neck and stares straight ahead when she walks. That's Roop.'

Or, 'That's Shahnaz. Easy to spot. Hippo hips.'

I didn't like that and said so.

'Okay, Sabina. I understand. Never explain from a man's perspective.' He had laughed at me. Because I knew women would also know her from her girth and her rolling gait. In time, I would guess in the same way.

I thought about my mother-in-law's walking style. Would I recognise her? Had I paid attention? Did she 'waddle like a duck', another of Riyaz's observations. Did her gloom escape her shroud and drag at her feet? Actually, no. Outside the home she walked purposefully, utilitarian sandals swatting the ground. Remember though, she was not on an *outing*. Never. She was doing errands. An outing for the sake of it, like I jaunt off on, would be *frivolous*.

Am I too fun-loving? It's a question I've begun to ask but there isn't really an answer. Am I to become pinched with endless cooking and dusting? Is that my future? To have plump babies and be a more docile woman?

My mother-in-law's only visits to other homes are to offer condolences when acquaintances have died, suitably solemn occasions which don't require a smile. When my mother noticed that my mother-in-law couldn't smile at me, even on my wedding day, she took me aside. 'Be patient and calm to all you meet in your new home.' Well, there was only one other person in my new home other than Riyaz so I understood the reference. She added, 'You made your bed, you must lie on it.'

Ah, bed. Lying on a bed with Riyaz. That is what I'd wanted. I wanted it to be sanctioned. I wonder why approval mattered so much.

*

Riyaz and I hid our love. On late afternoons, he would wait some distance from the college and we would walk together by the canal, talking, before he returned to work. We did not walk hand in hand. If I touched him, if I tried to brush even the tips of his fingers, he would move away from me. 'Not here; not in public.'

He was right, but I sulked. Sometimes we passed a policewoman walking in the other direction on the canal path. She'd be carrying a striped canvas bag filled with vegetables and fruit. Riyaz would nod at her. 'That's Amna. Off-duty now. On her way home.' Her face was veiled in a khaki scarf and she wore the police uniform of khaki tunic and trousers. He'd smile indulgently at my questioning frown. 'She lives in the old town. I know her. Of course I recognise her even in her uniform and with her face covered.' Amna would nod back politely. I felt her eyes on me, perhaps identifying me as a student. Riyaz told me that the road outside the college gates was within her patch. Occasionally I saw her too, on the road, dealing with accidents, stopping suspected criminals with her team, or on a quiet day, just sorting out the traffic jam. She never spoke to me. Riyaz said it was because she was a discreet woman and good at her job. She must see a lot that she would never talk about to anyone in the old city.

In those days, when my parents drove out of town to visit my sister and her baby, I would smuggle Riyaz into my bedroom after dark. He'd leave before dawn. Before he left, I'd mark him. Deep streaks with my nails. His shoulders, his upper back. If there was another woman, I wanted her to know about me. Riyaz would surrender to my immature clawing, even as he whispered, 'There's no need, Sabina, I tell you there's no need for this.'

One night I'd had enough. I sat at the dining table, sipping tulsi tea. I'd switched off the lights but the yellow glow from the hall was enough to see the shapes of the pot, the mug, the table. The shape of Riyaz as he crept in, knelt by my chair.

'What is it?' he asked.

'I want to lie with you in *your* bed, in *your* home, *every* night.'

'My home is not like yours. It's… different.'

'I know. I can adapt.'

'You haven't even seen my home.'

'Then show me.'

'You will change your mind.'

I know how tightly I held his face. 'How will I change my mind about you? Don't you understand anything?'

He rose and sat on a chair next to me. 'I will take you to meet my mother.'

*

He wasn't the only one who tried to dissuade me from marrying him. My closest friend said, 'I like him. He's a practical man. He's slightly older than us so he knows more of the world, and he's astute. If he himself tells you marriage isn't a good idea, you're not going to mind me telling you. You're crazy. Stupid crazy.'

'Love-crazy?' I asked.

'That's the same as stupid-crazy. How does it make sense for a smart, free-spirited woman to choose to live in the old city? You're used to doing as you please. You know what's going to happen.'

Love is illogical. If it was logical, it wouldn't be love. Rumi said: 'Love risks everything and asks for nothing...' But the latter part was not true of me. I risked and I made demands.

That first time I came to this house. I removed my outer layers, newly-bought, and Riyaz's mother invited me to sit by her on the sofa. She looked me over carefully and at the end of the inspection, her eyes rested pointedly on my fingernails. I turned them into my palms in silence. They were clean, medium length, unvarnished. Guilt must've risen in my face. I hadn't considered that she would be the woman who'd see the scratches I'd inflicted on Riyaz. When? Had she noticed during the summer? In the heat-wave his abrasions had become itchy and swollen and he'd had to dab calamine lotion on them regularly. He told me he couldn't wait to take off his shirt and at home he wore only a singlet. He'd been so uncomfortable that I'd resisted with my jealous habit until the monsoon hit and he healed.

On that first visit to what would be my new home he was as nervous as I was. 'Let me show you upstairs where my room is.' He led the way.

His mother followed. She watched me as I looked around his bedroom.

'If you tell me what you want,' Riyaz said, 'I will get everything done as you like, before the marriage.'

'It's very nice.' *Lie.* 'There's no need to change anything.' *Everything would have to go.* 'I'll be just fine.' *I would do the makeover once I was installed.* I wanted to give no excuse to his mother to say an unkind word about me before the wedding. I feared that in her eyes I was wanton. I didn't know then she'd label me frivolous.

She was a woman who felt twice-betrayed by fate and who wore her misery on her sleeve. Her husband had died young. Her daughter, brought up in the old city, had rebelled against all the restrictions. She lived in Paris and visited every few years.

I knew it would be no use to quote Rumi to her: 'Escape from the black cloud that surrounds you. Then you'll see your own light as radiant as the full moon.' Young though I was, I'd begun to see that not every woman grew as wise with age as my own mother had.

Riyaz, however, was full of loyal praise for his mother. Before I'd met her he'd told me: 'My mother is an intelligent woman. She's perfectly fluent in three languages.' 'My mother is talented with her hands, she embroiders beautifully.' 'My mother is a fantastic cook.'

Not once did he say, 'She's an unhappy neurotic person who will hate you.'

Why hadn't he warned me? When he too noticed after our *nikah* that she couldn't smile for us, he took me aside just like my mother had done a few minutes earlier. He brought my hands up to his heart. 'I will make you happy, Sabina, I promise.'

*

A few weeks ago Riyaz took me to high tea at the newly restored palace of the nawab that was now a hotel. He asked his mother to accompany us.

'I've seen the palace,' she sniffed. 'I've seen it a million times. It's as dilapidated as my life.'

'You haven't been inside since it was restored,' he cajoled. 'It's only just opened. Come with us.'

'I don't like lah-di-da manners.'

'Just have a cup of masala tea there if you like,' he pleaded. 'You'll be able to point out what they've got wrong in the restoration.' Riyaz knows how to amuse her. He's a very good son.

'You go. I'll have my tea at home.'

At the palace gates, I rolled my *burqa* into my bag and went in on Riyaz's arm, in a floor-length dress and a gauzy scarf on my hair. Tea was served on a shady terrace. Huge butterflies flitted in the shrubs around us. The china was white and dainty. I was slightly bemused. I wanted colours and patterns, but the cups, saucers, teapots, milk jugs, everything was plain white. Even the slim white vase that held the vivid purple blooms of an orchid. Riyaz said I could take the flower out of the vase and take it home.

'Don't be silly.' But I touched it. Stroked it.

Unusually, he enjoyed the high tea more than I did. I found the cakes too creamy, too chocolatey. He gorged on the open cucumber sandwiches. He ate both our portions of scones with clotted cream and rose-petal jam.

I remember he'd so relished the tea that he'd told the waiter, 'We're definitely coming back.' I didn't realise I was gazing into the distance as I walked.

'You're dreaming about food, aren't you?' Sometimes Riyaz guesses what I'm thinking. 'Shall we go back to the palace hotel for their Nawabi dinner for our anniversary?' He stops for a moment at the Bangle Bazaar junction. 'Thirteen courses, remember that mouth-watering menu?' He touches my elbow. 'Let's not think about how many thousand rupees it costs. That's what you're dreaming of, right?'

Wrong. Although food is part of the Goa dream if I take into account the prawn curry. I stay silent. He walks on. 'I'll need to eat something quick. I must return to the office soon. What should we share, Sabina?'

'Nothing. I don't want to eat. I'm not hungry.' My stomach clenches in disbelief at my words.

He stops again. 'You must eat lunch.'

'Don't tell me what to do. Do *not* tell me what I *must* do.'

'You told me you would adjust, remember? You insisted that you could-'

'*Don't* remind me of my mistakes.' I place my hand on his cheek. It lands as a light slap. Half-joking, half-meant. My anger has bubbled out suddenly, taking me by surprise.

We hear a camera click. A tourist has snapped the moment. Riyaz looks at her, she's a few feet away on a side street, under a shady awning. His face darkens. 'You shame me in public, *begum*.' He crosses the road to a *biryani* stall, leaving me standing alone. I wait. He returns holding a paper plate heaped with vegetable rice. He begins to eat, motioning to a spare fork.

'Eat.'

'No.'

I know how I punish him. He deserves it. He would hop off to his office. I would return to an afternoon of my mother-in-law's complaints. My life of restraints.

We part at the next crossroads. I watch him for a few moments, tenderness and anger roiling in my heart. I realise he's not heading out of the old city. I call to him, he turns.

'Why are you going that way?'

He walks back. 'I'm going to the flower stall. I want to see if he has anything interesting today.'

He can tell I'm beaming even though my face is veiled.

*

One evening last week we retired upstairs to our bedroom early. When I snuggled up to him, he withdrew a carefully wrapped flower from his jacket pocket. A purple orchid. He didn't hand it to me though. When I was half undressed and lying on the bed, he placed it between my breasts, sliding the stem under my bra at the front. 'Keep your bra on.'

He kissed the contours of my bra and the outline of the flower.

Before he settled into sleep he plucked the orchid from me and slid it under his pillow.

I wonder what flower he'll find today. Will I be as pleased if it's just a common marigold? How would that look between my breasts?

I quicken my pace. Daydreaming and dawdling are frivolous activities. I almost bump into the woman walking ahead of me. She's in a thick cotton burqa. I recognise the blue stripy bag stuffed with groceries. Half-day, Amna? I think. You're home early. I slow down to walk behind her. All this time, the policewoman been under my nose and I've taken her for granted. She crosses the invisible barriers of these lanes each day. Somewhere on the fringe of the old city there must be a spot where the auto-rickshaw drops her off and she slips on her outer garments before proceeding home. Does she hastily pin the *niqab* over her khaki scarf? Aren't you overheated and stifling, Amna? No. She walks coolly wherever she is.

I'm reminded of Amna's beat and where I want to be. Would I be fulfilled then, at the women's college? I have Riyaz, I have marriage and a home with him, what if I had academia too? If I followed the rules like Amna did, could

I live a dual life: inside and outside the old city? Would my resentments towards my husband dissolve?

I'd have to bear the barbs, that's all. If Amna could, I could. Like the proverb states: Sticks and stones may break my bones but words will never hurt me.

Once home I hurry up the stairs to my bedroom. My mother-in-law is already calling from the kitchen. I'm starving but I can't go down and scoff something straightaway. How to explain why I didn't eat with Riyaz? I'll have to wait till five, till tea. I delve in my bag for the packet from Faroukh. Those delectable coconut cookies crumble in my mouth; they'll have to keep me going.

I rummage in my cupboard to find the bra I'm looking for. In the early evening I'll wash off the dust of the day and change my undergarments. I'll wear something lacy this evening, something to take Riyaz's breath away.

If I get time to myself before he comes home and before we have dinner, I'll start the PhD application on my laptop. I may not mention it to him until later though. Maybe when he's very relaxed and about to sleep. I'll tell him about the second phone call from Mrs Palli and her invitation to return to philosophy.

SWEET PEAS

You sit outside in a rickety chair by the banana palm and watch the last of the drizzle roll into a tight waterdrop at the edge of a leaf and prepare to drip on to the ground. You like to watch the water drip, the people pass by. The neighbour tying and un-tying the knot on his *mundu*, his legs thin and not hairy enough; he goes past your chair with a nod. The girl with coconut oil in her hair, too much oil, you want to tell her, too much, and does she wash her hair often enough? Because sometimes you can see lice flakes on her long plait. The two unmarried sisters whose skins don't wrinkle or bag. For sixteen years you've watched them sashay past in their colour-coordinated saris, you've peered into their faces with an inquisitive eye but their skins have never lost the old lush beauty. How do they do that? If they knew, if you knew, somebody would have distilled their secret into a bottle and made a fortune.

This chair you're sitting on has been rickety for sixteen years, but you don't throw anything away until it breaks, until it is fully unfunctioning, and that's the reason you're not on the scrapheap yourself. Not kaput, not yet. You don't know how long you could go on sitting here in your daily meditation, and neither do the passers-by. They've come to terms with the apparition of you just as you have. 'That's the old man who says he's roamed the world. The one who says he's been rich in other lands. He thinks he knows everything.' They toss their heads to dismiss you, two steps after they've passed you, two beats after they've thrown you a toothy smile.

When you stopped working on the merchant ships, when you stooped to tinkering with the engineering of smaller vessels, when finally you snubbed going out on the little boats - on those puny soap-dishes, when you stopped sailing in all its forms, you decided to retire here, to your hometown, because the tip of South India was where you were born and where you thought you should return to die. There are days you regret your decision, but the new habits you have fallen into keep you going. You emerge at ten in the morning, washed and dressed, position your chair exactly ten paces from your front door and sit still, forming waves with your hands. You may look silly but you pay no heed. The waves you don't want to crest are those in your head. You can sit here by the banana palm for the remainder of your life and no one need know about the unrest inside you.

People are kind. This is something you have always believed. Lalitha, next door, calls you in to share fresh *appam*, whenever she makes them, which is infrequently now because, like you, she can't eat too much herself, and her children and grandchildren seldom sit down together with her. She grumbles that family meals are a rarity, but you know that in some parts of the world three generations eating together twice a week is an extraordinary occurrence.

You tell Lalitha that. In fact, you tell her all manner of things. You've even trusted her with your Big Idea. At eighty-two she has a handful of years on you, and you can rely on her to be discreet. You tell no one else of your Big Idea. 'Cruise ships as fully-functioning old-age homes.' It makes you chuckle to think that unofficially this may already be the case, some of the time, on certain cruises, but your idea is a serious one. You want a proper set-up. Quality and high standards. A hospital ship with a difference. Cruise liners: the old-age homes where you are still going somewhere.

Imagine that. Not the end of the road, not the way a care home tucked away on an English country lane really is the end of the road. Not the 'I'm so helpless now, admit me here to die' scenario. No, you're thinking more of the 'I'm so hopeless now, do send me on a cruise, darling' scenario. You're dreaming of the endlessly changing views of the ocean. Lalitha says, 'Doesn't it look the same, for days at a time? Sea today, sea tomorrow. Blue. Grey. Blue.'

You concede that to an undiscerning eye it could look the same for days. But even so, there is scope for change, you tell her, scope for land to jut into your horizon, beckoning your eye; scope for ambition. A chance to say, 'I'll stay alive till I set foot on *that* piece of land.' As opposed to, 'Should I stay alive for them to drip the same breakfast down my chin tomorrow?' Lalitha is unconvinced, but what does she know?

If there had been more money and vigour to back up all the big ideas you've had, well, you don't know where you'd be. On a cruise ship, at the very least. With carers to the left, carers to the right, carers behind...

When it comes to pass, as it will, who will know that the germination was here, in this rickety chair? The dream of the man with the thick white hair and vestiges of handsomeness in his jaw and lips. The man whose hands tremble like waves and over whose head hangs a small bunch of green bananas.

Lalitha asks about seasickness. About fuel. The environmental cost. She likes to put a spanner in the works, that's her personality. She likes to drill holes in your Big Idea. You snap at her that seasickness is not specifically an elderly affliction. The seasick population can stay away. What about cars and planes? Crammed on the roads. Creating a racket in the sky. Ships on water are a far better option. You wonder about her, about people like her. She's lived by the sea all her life but never ventured on to its deceptive surface. Not even on a soap-dish. From the bow of a boat you used to look at the contours of land, those daring protrusions into ocean, and you felt sorry for all the trapped people in the miles and miles that ran inland. From the boat it was easy to tell that the sea just tolerated the land.

You tell yourself that this harmless wandering in the inane parts of your mind is good for you. It keeps you out of the insane parts. Your big ideas keep you steering onward, or round and round, but nothing spills out, nothing spills out to mark the street. Because if you drift off course, if you let yourself drift towards the beginning, or the days when everything mattered, then you are consumed, and your mind is as a room overwhelmed by the scent of sweet peas; so strong it can make you sick.

In some parts of the world, you tell Lalitha, summer is a short-lived many-splendoured thing and the sweet peas are perfumed so as to make you gag. This is the kind of knowledge you impart to her quite smugly.

'Sweeter than here?' she asks, disbelieving again. 'Flowers smell more strongly than they do here?' She touches the purple flower pinned to her neat white bun and looks into the distance. 'Sweet peas grow in the coolness of the hills.'

'Not in England,' you explain. 'What I'm telling you is in the context of a short-lived summer. When long dreary months bring only the fragrance of damp bark and soggy grass, then filling a room with just-blossomed sweet peas from the garden can make you very ill.'

'It's always summer in Kotapuram,' she says, in placating mode.

'I like it better when you're angry,' she adds. This is what Lalitha says when she's afraid a strange sentimentality will drown you. She wants you to rage instead at unknown foreigners. Lalitha, whose face and body are shrinking by the day, wants you to bang on the rosewood table and bawl out your furious questions, as if you'd been transported elsewhere, shouting at people in other lands: 'Why do you take no notice of the sea? Of what it has brought to you? The cars you drive. The toys you break. The tea you drink. The beef you eat. The Christmas baubles you hang up. The gadgets that fill your rooms. Containers and containers and containers wending their way on water.'

None of this is relevant to Lalitha. You wonder if this is why she prefers it when you're irate, when you swing your palm down to slap the rosewood and stop reminiscing about the nauseating sweet peas of an English summer.

TIPPING POINT

DAY 7 of my new existence. I have a plan to make it bearable and this evening my little project has worked perfectly again. If I can go on a detour three or four times a week without my hosts suspecting anything then there will be delight in the world, harmony in the star charts, new hives for bees, and funding for the Arts. Et cetera.

I am already in the bedroom, changing out of my work-shirt and into a t-shirt, when I hear them come in. My office shoes are in the hall but a female voice floats upstairs anyway: 'Mee-heer, are you home?'

'I'm home,' I call back. Not that this is my home; it's hers and she's letting me stay as a house-guest until I find a flat I want to rent. I've been here a week. It feels like seven years.

'I'll get some dinner going,' she calls. I hear her say something to Atul that I can't catch.

I must go down to pretend to help. But I'm bushed. I'll lie down for just two minutes. Just. Two. Minutes. The bulb shines its yellow light into my eyes. The bulb is shaded by one of those round paper contraptions that were sold everywhere - Ikea, Habitat, John Lewis – in the last decade. Cara, whom I am learning to refer to as 'my estranged wife', with the emphasis on '*strange*', would never countenance such a lampshade. This particular once-white paper orb is covered in a film of dust. Cara would rip the thing down.

Has she arrived home yet? Has she found the open pizza box on the tiled path to our front door? Currently *her* front door. I have been manipulated into exile or 'am trying a new way of habiting', depending on whose viewpoint you want. It's a pepperoni pizza. The red of the pepperoni amid the yellow splodge of cheese picking up on the dark red tiles of the path. There's artistic vision in my plan.

Outside the window, the cloudy sky has darkened further into the smudged blue-black of Pantone 433C. If Cara is not home yet, then she's likely to surprise a fox eating the pizza when she does get back. I hope you make a real mess, fox; smear the pizza on the path, you diseased little fox. Cara may come home tired, but she'll bring out the mop to wipe off the goo. She may even have to slosh a bucket of water to get rid of the smell and get the tiles looking clean.

'Mee-heer.' What is it with the woman below? Why can't she pronounce my name properly? Mihir. Soft i, soft i. Mihir. Not Mee-heer. A bit much when I can pronounce her name correctly. First vowel, barely enunciated, second vowel, long *e*, as in eek.

'Yes Denise?'

'Dinner's ready.'

We sit at Denise's kitchen table, Atul, Denise and I. Looking at my hostess who has kind eyes and frumpy shoulder-length hair, I'm reminded of what Cara once said about her. 'You can tell she's not a creative person,' she'd said.

'How?'

'There is no spark of it, no flash of it in the clothes she wears or the furnishings in her house. So, well, if she is imaginative, it's well hidden.'

'She could *do* inspired things rather than just look artistic.'

'But we know her. She doesn't *do* creative.' Cara had shrugged. 'It doesn't mean anything. Denise is one of the most likeable and dependable people I know. That's what's great about her.'

I pile a mound of dependable Denise's penne with sundried tomatoes and tinned tuna on to my plate.

'I steamed some broccoli for you, Attle,' she says, too sweetly, pushing a plate of the greens towards him.

Okay, she can't pronounce her own husband's name. Why haven't I noticed this before? But then we have never spent a week living under the same roof. For me, it is already too long. And who knows? Possibly for them too. It's not like Cara and I are known for our easy-going qualities. But Atul was so welcoming when I arrived and he and Denise are making a real effort to coddle me. Atul is my best mate, after all. Even so, he'd looked shocked to see me wiping down the skirting boards on the staircase on my second day as house-guest; Sunday, incidentally.

'What are you doing?' he'd gasped. I'd tried to explain. Cara couldn't bear dust gathering in crevices. Because of Cara, and having lived with her for far too long, although less than seven real years, I was programmed to clean when I saw grimy skirting boards. It was Cara's fault.

'But I'll stop now,' I'd said. Then I'd waited for them to take themselves off to their bedroom for weekend conjugal relations before I'd surreptitiously crept out to finish the job. I'd already cleaned the skirting boards in my room and the tiny guest shower-room. For the grooves I'd used a toothbrush, the one Denise had given me on the first night, when I'd arrived after phoning Atul to ask if I could stay a few days. As if I'd storm out of my house without my own toothbrush.

I'd hit on the pizza plan on Tuesday. All day at work, instead of coming up with a new design for the lettering on Stavio's fat new highlighter pens, I'd wondered how to get at Cara. Driving back to Atul's place in Balham instead of my own quiet road in Putney I'd been overtaken by a pizza delivery idiot skittering his purple moped on the road. He almost crashed into a traffic island before wobbling right in front of my car forcing me to choose between braking hard (not good for the car) or killing him. I raised two fingers at him. He raised four back. But the moron had given me an idea. I u-turned then and there, paid out five pounds for a foul take-away pizza, drove home, to *my* home, and threw the open box on the path, letting the pizza slither out. Greetings, Cara.

DAY 13

I think the plan is working well. I have mashed pizza on the path a total of six times. I have thought about hanging around to see her reaction but it would be too risky. I would love to see her scrubbing those tiles. This is exactly the sort of minor annoyance that would drive her up the wall. I know the mess is being cleaned up, but I want to know for sure that she is getting as worked up as I expect her to. But then I wonder what I will do if I go to spy on her and see that she's ignoring that evening's pizza slop; that she's sitting on the sofa instead, feet encased in her knitted bootees, legs up on the stool, watching Miss Marple on TV with a glass of chilled white wine in her hand. (I can't stand white wine.) But of course, I wouldn't be able to look in anyway, because Cara always closes the curtains before she sits down to watch TV. And what excuse would I give Atul and Denise? Going out is fine, they are gagging for me to go out, but presumably I should have a plausible story. If I was sighted hanging about my own home by a passing busybody, they might mention it to Cara, who would then put two and two together. As it is, I stop by in haste now, parking a few doors down, and don a cycle helmet and bulky yellow jacket, so that even if neighbours happen to be looking out, they won't really be able to tell who it is in the early evening darkness.

Happily, at dinner tonight (*farfalle* with asparagus and olives), I do get confirmation that all is not well in Cara-land. Denise starts to speak in a confidential, soothing voice. 'I spoke to Cara today.' She waits for a reaction. I give her none. Atul glances at me and I look blankly back at him to show it's cool with me.

'What does Cara have to say?' Atul asks his wife in a non-committal tone. Translation, which we can all hear loud and clear: Hey babe, go easy, don't upset my friend or by extension, me.

'Cara's a bit distressed, but I mean, not about this' – Denise waves her hand apologetically around the table – 'but something else entirely.' She widens her hazel eyes. 'She's being picked on by some local teenage gang.'

I feel a twinge of worry for Cara, but it subsides. Denise looks at me as if I should be rushing to Cara's aid. But I am living here now, Denise, see? I'm not Cara's minder.

'What gang?' Atul asks. 'Why?'

Denise carries on with her story in a calming, I-was-made-for-counselling voice. 'Apparently, a couple of weeks ago, she reprimanded these three youths who were standing on the pavement just outside her house throwing beer bottles at passing cars. She told them to stop. "Yeah, what's it to you," one of them sneered. "It's not right," she told them. "Don't do it." And then she backed down a bit and said, "Don't do it standing here, anyway. Go elsewhere for your fun game." They left, but they made a throat-cutting gesture at her as they did so.'

I'd heard this story from Cara the day it had happened. I'd told her to call the police if she wanted; she'd grunted as if that was a useless suggestion. That was the week every conversation was actually a quarrel. No matter what I said, I got a snort in reply. It went on all week, till late on Friday night I packed my bag. 'I'm taking the car,' is all I said by way of goodbye. She'd grunted.

Denise continues with her account. 'She thinks they're targeting her now. She said that for the past three days *in a row* they've left a stinking half-eaten pizza on her front path.'

Atul frowns in puzzlement, I try to imitate his expression. 'Is she sure it's the kids?' he asks finally. 'A gang is wasting eight bucks a night on terrorising her with *pizza*?'

Not eight, five pounds, I want to say. Not fancy pizza, Atul. These low-grade ones cost under a fiver. I keep my lips sealed, even press them inwards in sympathy at this outrage to my ex-front-path.

'Well, she's not completely sure, but she guesses it's those local youths she had an altercation with. Attle, that's why I've offered your help.'

'What?'

'Well you know, since we're friends with both of them' – she nods towards me – 'we must treat them fairly. With equal support. I'm sure Mee-heer will agree.'

Mee-heer won't, but no one is asking Mee-heer really.

Denise is using the counselling tone again. '*He* is staying here so I thought we should offer Cara our support too. It's a difficult time for everybody.'

Not least for you, I think. I have been your uppity guest for almost a fortnight.

'What kind of help have you offered Cara?' Atul asks, sounding a bit desperate.

'Well, I said that you could stake out their home, just for a couple of evenings. If you parked there, say from 4 onwards until Cara got back, you would see who's leaving the pizza. You'll have a description. You might even be able to get a photo.'

'Jesus, Denise, I'm busy. I don't have time to sit around in cars, waiting for loons to show up.'

'Just a couple of days. Not tomorrow, obviously, it's too short notice. But you could arrange it. Next week, Monday or Tuesday?'

'Jesus, Izzy. Hire a PI.'

When she doesn't respond, he says, '*You* do it.'

He gets a look. You know, the wifey look. The one that brooks no argument.

He glares at me. What did I do? Then Denise turns to me too. 'Unless you want to help, Mee-heer. Although' – she delicately wrinkles just the top of her nose – 'Cara did say she wanted to have nothing to do with…'

'Ya, ya, I'll go one afternoon next week,' Atul interjects quickly.

The Planet Spins On Its Axis, Regardless

I take the dishes to the dishwasher and stack them on the counter. Denise stands there like she's waiting for me to do something. Like a schoolteacher's stare when you haven't quite finished a task. She *is* a schoolteacher, so this must be the look her pupils receive – strict but kindly, hint of twinkle, hint of steel. I get it. I'm meant to put the dishes in the dishwasher. Cara could never tolerate a stranger – well, a newbie – in the house filling the dishwasher. There are only certain ways the bowls are allowed to go in. And the large plates are always on the left; the small ones on the right. Two spoons of the same size do not sit together. They never get properly clean if you do that. Wooden-handled knives *never* go in. How is it people don't know that? The inside of Denise's dishwasher is haphazard. As I re-arrange the breakfast dishes so that I can stack the dinner plates the right way, I think about Atul staking out my home, or Cara's home as it is now, next week. That's Plan One brought to an effing halt.

I slide in the dishwasher racks and close the door. What I can do is finish Plan One on a high. A proper blast. Five pizzas, why not? Three squished into the path for smelly gloop on Cara's heels; two upturned to show their colours when she switches the porch light on.

DAY 24 as house-guest. Dinner is a stilted affair. Atul and Denise are fidgety, their eyes skating over me but also not quite meeting each other's. I wonder if they know about the five pizzas. Do they want to accuse me but can't bring themselves to, despite instinctively grasping the truth?

Denise fairly chucks dishes on to the table. I wheeze in surprise. It's not pasta! We've got brown rice and chicken breasts and spinach. Denise nudges the plate of spinach over to Atul's elbow. He's been ignoring it studiously, but nudge by nudge it has come closer and is almost being pushed onto his place mat. He gives in; he helps himself to some and then pushes the dish away with a quick roll of his oval eyes. I've already served myself a healthy helping and as I look down at the wilted spinach on my plate I feel a cramp of sorrow in my stomach. Atul, a samosa-and-parantha man who believes 'if it ain't fried, it ain't got no taste', is being looked after. These veggies that Denise thrusts on him are a form of her love. I swallow and stab my fork into my spinach.

It is up to me to provide some sparkling conversation to lift the mood, but I find I can't. I have spent the last few days gnawing weakly at life. I've stayed late in the office, texting Atul to say I'll be home after 10 pm. I've eaten crisps at my desk. I don't want pubs or people. So the three of us sit quietly, lost in our own worlds, our mouths chewing in unison. After we've cleared up and I've scrubbed the pans to make them look dazzling new, Atul invites me to sit back down at the table to finish the bottle of wine, it being manic Monday and all. Denise says she'll leave us to it. I sense that they've planned this. She offers me an explanation, saying she wants an early night because she's fasting the next day.

Atul swings round in unfeigned surprise. 'Fasting? For what?'

'Your mother rang to remind me. It's *Karva Chauth* tomorrow.'

'Already? Again? So soon?'

'Yes.'

'You don't have to fast, Izzy, you can just ignore Mum. I'll tell her you didn't eat till you spotted the risen moon.

You stood outside, wearing your wedding bangles, peeping through the sieve, waiting. Ha. As if you'll even be able to see the moon through the clouds.'

'Oh no, don't lie to her,' Denise says. 'I don't mind, really.' For the first time this evening she actually looks into his face. 'I quite like the idea: fasting for the well-being of my husband.' She is all liquid eyes and tender mouth. Atul puffs out visibly, his chest growing an inch and his neck straightening up.

'Goodnight Denise,' I say as she wafts upstairs in a warm glow.

Atul pours out wine, insisting on fresh burgundy glasses. Is he becoming like me? The dishwasher makes its swilling sounds in the background along with an erratic rumble or two. The tension in the room has melted and we sit companionably.

'Mihir, *yaar*,' Atul asks me softly, 'how's work going?'

'Great. Although I'm not concentrating as much as I should I suppose. I'm re-designing the labels for XT shampoo; guess what, instead of cylindrical clutchable bottles we're moving to elongated trapezoid containers. Big deal, huh? Didn't get any sample labels done today but I'll knock out a couple of ideas tomorrow.'

'Good, good.' He lets me slurp down some more wine. 'And how's the flat hunting going?'

Atul is such a sweet guy that I know this is the closest he will come to telling me my time is up. I must leave him and Denise in the peace they deserve. I feel sorry for him. But before I speak, he hurries on. 'You know if you want to talk about... Cara – or what happened, or your... feelings – you can, I mean, I know how to listen...'

'Thanks, *yaar*,' I say and feel red wine dripping out of the side of my mouth.

In their guest room I lie back on the small bed and stare up into the deep yellow light of the bulb, which gently illuminates all the dust on the paper shade that surrounds it.

It was kind of Atul to ask. But what can I tell him? Cara, obsessive-compulsive Cara, is bored of marriage. Been there, done that. She wants to live on her own, despite the mad youths and the burglars. I can't tell Atul that this came about after our last trip to India for my sister's wedding. Cara was surrounded by these jumped-up pumped-up Bombay boys. Maybe she's dallying with one of them. Maybe all that interest turned her head.

What I do know is that everyone can see I've been wronged, yet it's Cara who steals their sympathy. I will move out from here soon; heck, I'll have chosen a flat by next week. My temporary needs are simple. A one-bedroom place, freshly painted. A window that overlooks a green space: a communal garden or a park or someone else's well-tended garden.

The problem with living alone after some years of cohabiting is going to be this: who do you blame for what your life has slid into? Who do you blame for the lethargy, for the visits not made, for the sarod that sits reverentially in its own corner not being played? Marriage is an institution that turns you into a round shape sinking into a round hole.

Now that I have to acquire protrusions, who do I blame if I remain a round peg submerged in a round hole? The world will close up above me forgetting I am there. I won't remember anyone's birthday and no one will remember mine. The old Mihir I knew has already been erased.

The Planet Spins On Its Axis, Regardless

Everything is Cara's fault. I try an experiment to prove my hypothesis. I pull myself up to sitting and I throw my socks, one by one, across the room. I lie back down. I last three seconds before I am compelled to sit up and fetch them. I was always tidy. People occasionally said that I was obsessively tidy but those people had never met Cara. Once you'd seen Cara's standards, you would know that I was only in the middling league of such behaviour. Of course, despite her hygiene-and-order fixation, or because of it, Cara gets sick all the time. I place my socks on the carpet again, but this time in the spot I have assigned for them, by the roller suitcase I brought with me, and I sink back on the bed, feeling better.

Everything in its place. First, I find the right flat. Second, I think of another way to madden my estranged wife. A purposeful life is a good life.

A FLASH OF PEPPER

Carrying a single bag, the young man is travelling alone at his whim with no particular destination in mind. These are the times when fantastic things happen, when he is likely to be discovered, or he will stumble upon people and places that affect him forever. When he takes the day off from life, from window-cleaning, and instead of lazing in a yum-cha place he heads out to far corners of his buzzing city, that's when life with its wonders and weirdness will find him, it will come barrelling at him with its surprises.

That was the theory. It was not quite how it was working out today.

The satchel slung loosely from the young man's shoulders and though there were spaces to sit on the MTR he decided to stand by the door. At each station he'd wondered whether he should get off the underground train and change lines, then take a bus to somewhere in the New Territories. But he hadn't been quick to make up his mind at the last three stops and now the train sped through long blackness to the other side of the shrinking harbour. At the first stop on Hong Kong Island he escaped the train and rode upwards on a random escalator, upwards into the open air. This was better.

He followed a woman who had been on the step ahead of him on the escalator. She moved purposefully towards a walkway stretching between buildings. He didn't think much of her dress sense: black skirt, black blouse, white cotton cardigan, black pumps with a white bow. He had aunts who dressed like that, maybe it was an eighties look, something these ladies had not grown out of yet.

He himself liked to dress carefully, although he only had the one style. T shirt, jeans, Converse trainers. The T shirt was always fresh for the day, his hair was always clean, also his face, his ears, his nails.

The lady he'd followed was heading into an office tower. He took up the footsteps of a person who seemed to be a tourist; a tall man with matted blonde hair and a large backpack. The tall man led him to the ferry terminals for the outlying islands and the young man, Sze, decided that he too, could play tourist for the day, as he had occasionally done before. He had never visited the Big Buddha on Lantau Island and today would be the day. Nothing wondrous had happened yet, although last night as he looked out at the eerie glow of the flyover outside his window, he had thought that this day in June would be special somehow.

Last night the thought had come to him that the flyover was an alien land. Although about ten metres away from his vantage point, when he looked down at its bright loop in the darkness it was a space that offered a complete contrast to his room on the other side of the window. Sze lived on the twenty-first floor of 'Money Gardens', a collection of scruffy buildings for those with not that much money. There was certainly no garden. His bedroom had been the smallest in the flat to begin with, and on moving in his family had partitioned it with plywood into two narrow rooms, one for him and one for his grandmother. Each of them could fit a single bed and a cupboard into their allotted spaces. At least they didn't have to share.

Sze got the window because he asked first. His grandma spent most of the day sitting at the dining table from where she looked out of another window into the world directly below, mainly at the taxi rank. She preferred the activity and bustle of tiny people arriving and departing from Money Gardens, everyone so tiny, the taxis too, because she was looking down at them from this great height.

When Sze gazed at the flyover, which was so much closer, the cars were not small, and nor were they life-size. At night, the flyover was a plaything, an unreal world. The lamps cast a green glow that arced over the flyover's steep curve. Late at night the traffic thinned and he watched the long yellow splinters of headlamps appear first, beaming ahead and crisscrossing the green arc. Then there would be the whoosh, a short whoosh, and the car would scurry by just out of reach, seemingly just below his window, before looping out of sight. Last night he had stared at the strange lights and empty curves for a long time in a half-dreaming state and that's when he'd realised that the flyover was an alien land. One that belonged to the viewer from his window.

It was a small consolation. There was not enough money to go to a truly alien land, to other countries, unless the other country was China, which didn't count. All young people wanted to travel and see the world, it was natural. That's what all those Scandinavians were doing in Hong Kong, and what he wanted to do in their big, clean, cold and green lands. But if you couldn't get on a plane because you couldn't buy a ticket, or not yet anyway, not with the proceeds of window-cleaning for a clutch of shops around Money Gardens, all you could do was travel one day a month and see the sights of your own city. You didn't have to follow a tour guide or have a plan. You could step out and let the world find you. No one had had to tell Sze this. He'd thought of it himself.

His philosophy might seem fatalistic, but if so, it was still a positive philosophy. His father, who read faces for a living at a street market, had told him life and everything in it was all about interpretation. His father didn't earn much at the street market but hadn't been able to secure a spot at a big temple where he could charge a good price. Where he operated it was all about enticing tourists to pay twenty dollars for five minutes having their fortunes told based on the features they had been blessed with, or not; as the case may be.

Sze disembarked the ferry at Mui Wo and found the bus that would take him on its winding uphill route to the foot of the Big Buddha. He too, could find whatever it was other visitors found here. Last night, on discovering his own alien land outside his window, he had felt that a magical moment was blowing itself towards him. It hadn't happened yet, but it was only the afternoon and there were many more hours in the day.

As he started up the two hundred and sixty steps he realised the people climbing beside him were sniffing the air, thick with incense smoke and pine-scent, and talking of peace. They also talked of vegetarian food. And drink. Water. Water. The *gweilo* were sweating buckets. Sze, too, was perspiring but he was ascending languidly, not bounding. A sense of mystery propelled him at a gentler pace. Would the day hold anything for him at all?

The giant seated Buddha looked down at him in benevolent bronze. Sze liked the Buddha, he liked the lush trees and mountain shrubs that surrounded him, he liked the glitter of the South China Sea in the distance and he liked the planes gliding by in the sky, waiting to land, or taking their first circle before flying away.

He wasn't on a plane. He bowed thrice to the Buddha for the sake of his parents and grandma and he turned to retrace his steps downhill. Something flew by him. Something flamboyant. Something that lived a vivid reality compared to his own dull existence. A bright red dragonfly shone in the sun.

Sze stopped under the overhang of a cedar tree, its long green arm offering him tender shade. He had never seen a red dragonfly before. Sze knew a little bit about dragonflies, nature's most beautiful creatures. Not that they did much other than feeding and finding a mate. They just didn't have the time. As adults they only lived for two to six months in their final form. They could spend almost four years as nymphs in the water where they'd been laid before they emerged in their brilliant colours and gauzy wings.

He was not as fragile as a dragonfly. But could he be as stunning as the pepper-red one that had brushed him in flight? It was a resolve he could make. He could spend time looking good; maybe it was not such a shallow thing after all. Then, when opportunity knocked, as it would one day, he'd be ready for it. He would be ready for anything remarkable, when it happened.

COCOON LUCKY

It is December and I dwell on what fortune-tellers have told me in the past. There is not much else to do when 'festive season' occurs while we're in lockdown. I'm semi-shielding. Everything I do is half-baked and prefixed by semi or demi. Nothing is full-on, not even make-up for work Zoom calls or Zoom parties. Lipstick and a pearl pin in my unruly hair is enough, isn't it.

I'm trying to decide if I feel the need to go out or not. I'm quite content within my walls. I'm comfortable, thank you. I do like having walls.

The soothsayers of my past have a hit rate of fifty-percent in their predictions, which is what you'd expect. Some of them had rare imaginative detail, and it is that detail that made their predictions striking when something they said would happen, happened. One of them said I'd die abroad. I won't be able to comment on that one when it happens. Anyway, what is abroad?

Last year included travel to a beach. Last year in December there were festive happenings. I went along to a few Christmas drinks parties, but, one year on, they're hazy in my memory. I recall just one vividly. I remember walking into a buzzing room, getting entangled in my own coat as I attempted to hand it to the daughter of my friend, who was on coat duty, and accepting a glass of fizz from my friend's son, who was on drinks duty.

*

A knot of people are in intense conversation, and I join them because I know two of the six, so I can say 'Hello', and they can expand out to make space for me. I have inadvertently fallen into a very serious discussion about passports. After Brexit you know, they want to be sure that they, and their kids, also have European passports, so that they can all access Europe as Europeans – as well as being British, of course. Some of them were born in other European countries. Others have heritage. I am used to this; I have friends who are now also nationals of Ireland or Portugal, because one of their parents was born in those countries.

One of the men in the group is grumbling about how very long his new naturalisation process is taking. 'This is so important,' he says, 'and it's taking months. *Months*. My country can do better. It's the European leader in technology.'

'It's not,' another man cuts in. 'Finland is the nerdiest country in Europe. My country.'

'Aren't you American?' I ask.

He smirks. 'That's one of my passports. But I need a European passport now. This whole Brexit thing is so ridiculous.' Six people nod sympathetically at him. They all need a third or fourth passport for their children. Being British as well as non-EU nationalities is not enough, now, we need European papers too, for free movement.

I am possibly more sick of this talk than all of them, but that's because I find a passport a strange thing.

True identification of individuals is good, we need that for society and security. But to predicate movement on which passport one holds? When a passport can be the same as an accident of birth. One day we will have a different system.

I am tempted to talk about the refugees they have little sympathy for. Refugees are escaping something, hardship, at the very least, if not terror, and if they had the means they would waltz into Britain and buy citizenship like the planet's criminals do. One passport would do them. One right kind of passport. I don't say anything because we're at a party and two of them know my schtick anyway.

The others may have guessed my thoughts from the curl of my lip. One of them hard-nudges my arm in a friendly gesture, almost tipping my wine. 'Of course, these are first world problems,' she laughs.

I don't want to curb their discussion with my sniffy expression.

'I can't contribute much here,' I say, 'so please excuse me.'

I make my way to a white sofa and sit on it, attempting to affix a more pleasant half-smile on my face.

'Let's not be judgmental,' I say to myself. I know these are all lovely people. They are doing what they can to continue to prosper. They don't want any country that they live in to be overrun by the world's poor, that's all. And if they happen to belong (in mind, body and passport) to three countries, why then, they don't want the world's poor to overrun any of those nations. Sometimes I have asked them if some of those refugees might perhaps contribute more to the country they come to, than some of the 'born here' folks. Not that these people were 'born here', but as people with good fortune, it is different for them. They are always 'legal', aren't they? I ask them, sometimes, who provides all the things they love, such as dining out and embroidered garments? Who will provide the vaccine when it comes? Will it be former refugees, will it be 'foreigners'? Ah, I can be quite boring.

I can also be envious. Because I would've liked to have kept a passport that I had, oh, twenty-five years ago, but that country didn't allow dual citizenship. So I'm a one-citizenship gal.

I hope my half-smile is making me look pleasant and not a crosspatch.

It is Christmas and anger has no place in seasonal cheer. Nostalgia is permitted. Surfacing sorrows are allowed to zipline, everyone talks about losses at Christmas. An annual accounting that turns into a profit-and-loss table of years past.

I too, have affection for at least three countries, and heritage I can call on, but to gain one kind of freedom, I had to give up a part of me. You could say obtaining freedom of movement cost me the trusting part of my soul. I am suspicious of human beings the world over. I talk to animals, mostly domesticated or urban types.

I do talk to human beings. All I'm saying is I can be changeable. I can be the life of the party, but not this one. That first conversation I entered has plunged me into a soup of mixed emotions. Should I speak up? For the world? To the world? No, sit tight, sit quiet, love the life I have, don't complicate fragile comradeships.

The family's dog, a chocolate-brown labradoodle, who knows about unconditional relationships, sashays to the sofa to nuzzle me. 'Oh you've found me,' I say. Its tail wags and its eyes are alight with recognition. I'm the lady who dispenses long strokes. This is such a photogenic animal. It has posed so beautifully for the family greetings card. Last year the dog even sent its own Christmas card in addition to the family's one. It was signed. This is a dog with good handwriting and I'm on the favoured list.

I mutter up my gratitude to the universe for friends who offer good wine, classy canapés and a good-looking dog who acts as my sofa sentry, adding to my aura. I should be so lucky.

*

This Christmas I'm counting my walls and feeling cocooned. My walls are painted 'deep slaked-lime' chosen from an environmentally-friendly paint colour chart. I'm offering myself my own good wine and eating 'starters' from my grocery shop. These duck spring rolls apparently serve four people, but do me nicely as a meal for one. After a bit of clearing up I just have to toddle to bed and read my book.

Or I could answer my three hundred pending emails.

Or I could go for a walk.

I have been resisting evening walks this December. A strange inertia. Last year I walked home from that Christmas party that I remember so well. I even recall the walk home.

*

My neck is bundled in a red wool scarf. I've barely taken a few steps when a black cat detaches itself from the dark spaces by a fence and shimmies alongside me. 'At least you're not crossing my path,' I speak aloud to the cat and it doesn't run away. 'You're just bored and coming along for the walk home, looks like.'

All these superstitions about black cats – some good, some bad. What I believe depends on my temperament at the moment. Tonight, the cat is a good omen. In truth, a cat, black or not, is good. I've not yet found myself in a mood where I mind a cat crossing.

The cat meows and slinks so close to my legs that I can feel it. In a few minutes I'll be home. The new LED streetlamps are so white and bright. A fox crosses my path. It pauses to note my glance, and darts into darkness, into someone's garden or the children's playground.

'Alright.' I'm speaking to steady myself. There are good and bad superstitions about foxes crossing a person's path. Like with the cat, I usually take a fox as a good omen. It is living, it is doing its city thing. When I was a young girl, my grandmother used to let me dress up in her fox pelt stole, complete with fox's head. I have to say I loved it then. That was the first fox I'd seen – a dead preserved one. Now I regularly spot my local foxes, sometimes snoozing in the sun on the top of my neighbour's shed. Sometimes they startle me at night, like this one, that has crossed my path with a message, perhaps, and disappeared.

I realise I have stopped and so has the cat. I walk on and turn into my front door. 'Coming in?' I ask the cat. I go in and turn on the lights in the hall. The cat prowls around the front of the house, it's found something to interest it. I say goodnight and close the door on my harbinger of luck, hoping it sticks around. I already have some luck, that I have clawed for and clawed at over the years, but I can do with more. Who couldn't? When luck was a no-show I went about my business determined to greet it with open arms when it came. For many people it may feel like it never shows up at all, despite all the graft they put in. And in some life-stories, you do feel that ill luck has dominated.

It's hard to know if anyone else is as silly as I am, believing minute encounters to be visitations of luck. But believing in a universe that listens to my muttering is good for me, it allays the tedium of the perpetual striving that is life.

*

This Christmas season I'm finding excuses not to walk in the evening. Semi-shielding can be tiring. Just the constant deciding what not to do and what to do, organising enough food for the end-of-the-world (although will I be here to eat it?), and keeping up with what is allowed or when it will be allowed. My bubble-person is also semi-shielding, which makes two of us in a semi/demi state. In my holding pattern, I just wave to the neighbour's cat through the window. It sits on my sill, on the other side, its eyes flashing when they catch the light.

This December, I count my walls. I can eat in one room and work in another. I can sleep.

This December, in my dreams I'm vaulting about like a maniac at different latitudes and longitudes across the globe. Friends who are dead come to speak to me. My body lies tranquilly through this hectic adventuring. My body enjoys its familiar comforts, even in semi/demi state. It likes to be parked in its cocoon at home.

Home is where I have walls of my own to count. Anywhere else is abroad.

GALVANISE GLOSS

What if there has been no turning point in your life for the past twenty-two years?

You wait for something to spur you into a change.

There have been fluctuations, and movement, but no critical decisive moments. Never have you thought: *My Life Starts Now*. Not even when you decided to live alone after having spent ten years in different flats with a variety of flat-mates. That decision was easy; not pivotal. It was what you preferred and you are content on your own. But where is the big plot of your life?

You've believed in letting life unfold. Not for you frenetic stabs at this or that. Life has ribboned out, but rather distractedly. When you look up from the steering wheel of your imaginary buttercup convertible as it rolls along a green and pleasant land you don't see any huge signs marking junctions or routes you could take instead. The highway glides over vale and hill, then loops to you don't-know-where.

The bus you're actually sitting in this afternoon rolls on as you take in the cityscape from the top deck, third row. The bus is hibiscus red, the roads and pavements are grey but because it is summer and this year it *is* hot, people are a riot of colour. Those ditsy floral dresses, those linen shirts, those wide pastel culottes, those *man-sandals*.

The bus inches along the jammed road. They will pedestrianise this thoroughfare one day, the city mayor's office has a plan, but for now the street is rammed with shoppers. You are gazing down at the glitzy store windows when the slogan catches your eye. THIS LIPSTICK WILL CHANGE YOUR LIFE.

Who allowed that? The Advertising Standards Authority let that pass? Can a lipstick change your life? Heck, can it change anything?? Can it change your summer a teeny-weeny bit???

You lean forward, press the button so the 'Bus stopping' sign lights up with a ting. You disembark and run into the department store. You prowl the cosmetics counters looking for the brand emblazoned under the slogan. Brand L. Ah, there. The heat is making you crazy, 30 degrees in London, yes, it's making you pathetic, and making the pavements sigh, but never mind. You stand by the counter and say to the girl with triple-mascaraed lashes: 'I want to change my life.'

She's ready to serve but startled. Then amused.

'The lipstick?'

She's smart. She pulls out a tray of sample colours from the display stand and points to a row. 'Which shade would you like to try?'

'All three will change my life?' You sound like you're gasping for air, but actually your shoulders are shaking. You've begun to laugh in a way that is unseemly. You control yourself. You eye up the round smudges of sampling colours. Your finger hovers over a vivid pink. Let me guess, you think, Watermelon Squeeze? Candy

Too Sweet? Profound Rose? You have form here, you know about these things.

'This?' The sales assistant doubtfully dabs some of the rosy stickiness on your lips.

'Oh,' her voice rises in surprise, 'This bright colour does suit you.'

Who is she convincing?

'I'll take it. It will change my life. Lipstick can do that.'

She looks at you sharply; she can't tell if you're mocking the brand or cosmetics in general.

She rummages in a drawer while you ask: 'What is the name of this colour?'

She hands you a shiny packaged tube. You peer at it. *Judicious Use*. You give up, your shoulders heave and rock.

'Are you alright, darling?' A hand on your shoulder. She's not sure if you're crying or laughing. At this point you're not sure either.

'What kind of name is that?' You give a little hiccup. Perhaps a burp. But a hiccup would be more decorous. 'That's a stupid name for a lipstick.'

She holds out her hand for the offending item.

'Two years back I created names for lipsticks,' you tell her as you return it. 'It took hours, no, days, for one season's line. For brand Y.'

'That's such a good brand,' she responds.

'Pink Bluff, Poppy Chase, Catalina Nudie, now those are names for lipsticks. The brand founder loved the list I came up with.'

'Do you want to try another shade?'

'No!'

She retreats behind the counter but you can't stop telling her.

The Planet Spins On Its Axis, Regardless

'And then I did the next season. Jaisalmer Bride, Sahara Sky, Balinese Sunset. But I never felt like buying any of those lipsticks, you know. I just stuck to my usual.'

'Are you buying this? Is there anything else you'd like?'

'Daring Rosie, Bolder Goldie, Cheekier Mauve. I must have named forty lipsticks and glosses.'

She takes this as acquiescence that I'm a hooked consumer. 'That'll be twenty-one pounds, please. Do you have a store card?'

'Plum Perfection, Flawless Coral, Immaculate Sex.'

'Very nice indeed. Tap your credit card here please.'

'Then the founder-lady wanted something new. She liked to travel she said. So I came up with places with Y. To flatter her and her eponymous brand. Yakeshi, Yangon, Yamuna.'

'Do you need directions to anywhere else in the store? There's tea and cake in the café.' She gestures upwards.

What does she think? You're not an old lady who needs tea! You're only forty. Alright, plus two. 'York, Yaroslavl, Yazd.'

'The exit is that way,' she points. She hands you a cute little silver bag with your cute little lipstick in it.

*

When you go out the next Saturday, just for a wander in your area, you wear your perky 'Use Judiciously'. Who named this? How did they get away with it? Witty but c'mon. If it's going to be part of a *This Lipstick Will Change Your Life* campaign this name doesn't cut it. You wonder if you should've bought another shade, one with a better name! 'Slay Dragons.' Did somebody do that already?

You ask for your turmeric latte at the local café and you grin pinkly, 'Hi Naomi, am I stuck in a rut?'

'Hi.' The young woman at the till is drooping in the heat, but her smile stays cheery. 'I don't know you well enough to know.'

Oh my. A considered answer.

'Same order every time,' you point to your drink and your almond croissant.

'You're not the only one.'

It's too hot in the café. This never happens, but it's happening this July. You sit out on the bench under a tree, sipping, nibbling, perhaps nipping at life. Life is using you judiciously. It's not wearing you out or treating you bad. In your case it's just trundling along, not doing much. Perhaps leaving life to unfold was not the right move. But you trusted in life. And prayers. And now look.

An elderly couple seat themselves carefully on the bench on the opposite side of the road. A slight breeze rustles the leaves in your tree. Nice. You watch the couple. The lady's skirt flares, her varicose veins are out to catch the summer air. The man's short-brimmed straw hat barely keeps the sun off the red tip of his nose. They munch into their sandwiches. You smile at them, you feel indulgent. You might want a sweet man by your side were you ever to turn into a scented old lady, but you don't want to be them. Not him, not her. You want to be you. Changing your life, or not, one judicious lipstick at a time.

THE AFTERNOON AFTER

LAVENDER

She had square nails, unvarnished. She had muted hair – brown fleshed with light red, tendrilling to just below her shoulders. Under her ribcage, on her long waist, on the left, she had three beauty spots. There was no silicone in her breasts.

She kept a list on lined A4 paper. The list itself was folded into an envelope, which was tucked into the pages of a book which lay (seemingly carelessly, third from the bottom) in a stack of books, piled on the hearth of the small fireplace. The fireplace, unused since 1929, had small burgundy tiles, a metal insert and a painted wooden surround.

She bent down to retrieve the envelope from the book and fished out her list. There were eight names on the page. She had started the list when she was seventeen. In the intervening fifteen years, only seven names had been added. This was a selective list, this list of the men she might have sex with, at some clouded point in the future, should the conditions, weather and otherwise, be right.

Two of the early names on this list she had lost touch with. One had died. Of the others, she saw them once in a while, perchance, dictated by circumstances not of her doing. She herself had made no efforts: no calls, no valentine's cards, no scheming drinks get-togethers. Creating perfect conditions was not her forte.

Occasionally, she looked at this list. Very rarely, she added to it. Today was such a day, come after sparseness. She added the new name, from the evening before. Matthew Yeats. Yeats was not really his surname. For the purposes of the list, it's what she wanted to call him. Everyone on the list had a dead poet's name tagged on. She let the glow of excitement flood her, her breathing ragged. She savoured her moment, what a moment, the addition of a name to her list. Then she folded the lined paper, returned it to the envelope, and slipped it back into the old book, its pages yellowed within the blue binding.

MATTHEW

He had pale arms which had not been in the sun lately. Let's be honest, these were not the sinews of a gym fox who consumed protein shakes. These were slender arms. It was his voice which was honed to perfection. Cultured, well-modulated, finessed; it enticed and was never constrained by ums and ahs. He had dark hair curling all over the white sheen of his flat belly.

He, too, kept a list. His was on unlined paper and hidden in his desk drawer at home, under some invoices. His list was longer than hers. It named all the people he had ever slept with. But unlike Tracey Emin's installation he didn't include his brothers and sisters and childhood sleepovers. His was a 'scoring' list. It was a good, sound, multicultural, globe-trotting attempt.

This afternoon, he would look at it, that's all.

THE EVENING BEFORE

It was International Women's Day, March 8, and Lavender's friend, Xyla J, a professor of gender and sexuality was speaking at a forum. The crowd was large, comprised of other academics, friends, acquaintances and students, but it was growing restive. Xyla addressed them on one of her topics of expertise: the unfair burden. In brief, and generalising: women get paid less, do more, keep house, have and grow the children, all without sufficient support from the male population or the captains of industry or the government.

Despite her subject Xyla was the antithesis of what people call a "haranguing" feminist. She was immensely popular with colleagues, with friends, with students. She was the reason the lecture hall was bursting to its seams with a supportive, if fidgety, audience. Genders or non, sexualities or non, the human species was mostly represented. Xyla ended her talk and led a select group to The Dove and Elk pub nearby.

Matthew, like Lavender, was AFX. 'A Friend of Xyla'. Matthew knew her from her work at the Royal Geographical Society, where they were both honorary members of a fundraising committee.

At the pub, on a post-lecture high, Xyla continued to expound on how the gender order needed shaking up. Her cap of shining black hair fell forward emphatically in sync with her forceful statements. After a few minutes of this Lavender set down her beer and said wearily, 'It will not change. It will only change when nature takes a new step or science takes us forward. When men can conceive and will carry babies for nine months and deliver them and breastfeed them, then there will be the kind of gender equality you want. Till then, this is a futile cause.'

Lavender's comment caused big nods of approbation. Xyla looked at her with disgust in her dark brown eyes. 'That attitude will not solve anything,' she said. 'The question is how can we help here and now?'

But Lavender had sparked a tangential conversation on scientific advances; a topic sufficiently off-track from International Women's Day for it to be pounced upon by a group fatigued by the same old, the same old.

Xyla sat back and let the diverted conversation flow away from her for the moment. She knew how to wrest it back if she wanted. She watched her friend Lavender, how her long thin eyes rested on a particular man, rested at the spot where his shirt sleeve stopped, rested on his belt when he rose to get a round of drinks. Xyla awaited her opportunity.

In the midst of a discussion on increasing numbers of men signing up for cosmetic surgery, she heard Lavender say, 'You can't discount it completely just because you say you will never have it. You have to let those who have gone through it, those who believe they've benefited from such surgery, to speak for it.'

'Really?' Xyla interrupted, a false laziness in her voice. 'Actual experience counts for more than education, research and observation?'

Lavender, sensing the undercurrent of frostiness, was silent. But someone else, Matthew in fact, nodded enthusiastically at this pronouncement. To which Xyla added, 'So, Lavender speaks for nature to change or science to lead us forward before we can revolutionize the situation for women, but she herself has zero experience. She has never even had a boyfriend, that I know of.'

She turned to Lavender. 'Are you a secret siren?' she asked. 'Or could it be that you're waiting for the new dawn, the day males will conceive, and till then you will remain virginal.'

'Virginal,' someone spluttered, 'what a quaint word.'

'Virgin?' Xyla addressed Lavender, and it seemed a taunt.

'I leave you to your imaginings', Lavender responded breezily, as a secret siren would. After which Matthew leaned in closer and the evening hue became rosier. Xyla apologised to Lavender by way of a wink. Lavender, who was more aware of Matthew's arm pressed against hers, acknowledged the wink with a barely perceptible nod and no sign of a sulk. It was hard to hold anger against Xyla. In tandem with her razor tongue she bubbled with kinship on the human condition.

Speaking of conditions, they were almost perfect. But then the bar closed and when the group of stragglers found themselves on the wet street, they seemed to remember that tomorrow was another day and it was time to head home. Lavender had caught Matthew's sidelong gaze, but as ever, she was too shy to say anything. She was good at letting the right moment pass on by.

Matthew had darted another oblique glance at her, but said nothing.

'Virgin or siren,' thought Lavender, 'what did it matter, if they were going to be so daunted anyway?'

SHAMANS IN LUBURBIA

'I was told that if you smear the blood from your first period on your face you will never experience problems of severe pain or irregularity.' Pia made a face. 'Well, blow me down. What happened thirty-seven years later, huh? How many years have I suffered lately?'

'Did you do that? Smear the blood?' I'm trying not to sound too incredulous.

'Yes, not only that, the elder ladies in our village told me to put an onion under my left armpit and hop for five minutes every time on the first day of my menses and I wouldn't smell.' She sighs. 'I did that too, just for three months though.'

I giggle at the thought of immaculate Pia with an onion in her armpit. I'm curious to know more. 'Was this advice widespread in the Philippines or just in your village?'

'Don't know,' she says with a dainty shrug. 'If we'd had daughters instead of sons we wouldn't be imparting old wives' tales, would we?'

I consider. 'There were some traditions I might have passed on, even if I'm not sure about their efficacy. Rub a pure silver bowl on a girl baby's body. For smooth hairless skin. My mother said she did it for me.'

'But you weren't told anything about your first blood were you?'

'No,' I admit. I realise I don't know a single tradition about periods in India. Except that menstruating females, of any age, were not allowed inside the temples. The gods might be swayed by polluting blood and the impurity of womanhood; presumably they don't already know everything, they might be dishonoured, or distracted, as one priest put it. From what? From the fact of life itself? Distracted from being a god? The goddesses are apparently alarmed by menstruation too, because even in the temples dedicated to a powerful goddess, a menstruating woman is forbidden to enter. The idol loses her power if a 'live' power comes within her orbit. I mull over these traditions, thinking that, in truth, it might have made sense for women to stay home, as they did in every part of the world, until it became easier to remain active while on your period. Our gods and goddesses need to evolve with us – can someone tell the priests?

Pia is waiting for something from me. 'Nope,' I say. 'Can't think of anything to do with first menses. But maybe applying that blood on your face is your secret – you do have wonderful glowing skin.' I sound like an advertisement, but I mean it. At fifty-five her skin looks plump and soft.

She touches her face. 'That's just genes. Like you are long-limbed and your arms and legs haven't thickened.'

Pia doesn't say the rest of me has, she doesn't need to.

We glance at the pushchairs and four mums at the bigger table next to us. Our weekly brunch in this café, popular with new mothers, is her idea. Pia likes looking at the babies and remarking to me loudly 'thank god that's over'. She likes scrutinising her manicured nails and sometimes tossing her freshly shampooed hair. 'I was always a mess, never could get my act together to have my nails or hair looking good.'

I can't imagine her dishevelled but I nod. 'Me too,' I say. In my case, it wasn't just varnishing my nails that I never got round to, I couldn't be bothered dressing in anything that wasn't comfortable. It helped that my workplace dressing was casual too and I didn't often have to go into an office. That habit of comfortable clothes has persisted. I was always sleep deprived when my children were young. Since then sound sleep is the most beautiful sensation of all, even when I have an abundance of it.

We seem to have set something off at the next table because we're hearing stories of first periods from many different places. This is why I love eavesdropping and why I love London and also Luburbia. That's my name for our part of Greater London. We're in suburbia and in London, both. In Luburbia we are boastful about the fact we have a pond and a buzzing café life. Today, rows of cherry trees cheer up the grey sky. They thrust their blooms up, in their pink brightness and white delicacy, reaching up, above us, challenging the gloom the sky sends down.

The neighbouring table is in full flow about first periods, traditions and tales. The café owner, Alban, keeps his head down, but like us, he's listening. I learn from an ebullient talker among the mums that in South India in some communities a girl's coming of age is marked by celebration, she's given gifts and a half-sari. A half grown-up way of dressing. This is after she's isolated for a while, and this also means her period is 'announced'.

'The most embarrassing week of my life,' says the woman telling the story.

'At least you didn't get slapped,' someone pipes up.

'What?' the others shriek.

'We get slapped. My grandma slapped me. Only for the first period. It's the done thing.'

I can't tell where this tradition is from. I missed what the person said. Greece?

'I'd like to know what menopause traditions there are,' I growl at Pia.

Now she giggles like the sweet girl she must've been. 'Oh, as if you care. All we two do is moan about how terrible it is.'

Well, it has been for us,' I point out. Pia and I became properly acquainted in the waiting room of a hormone specialist. One morning I arrived for my first consultation, was shown to a seat, turned to my right and recognised the woman sitting beside me. Oh Horror. I knew her, sort of. We'd had a few clashes banging our trolleys at the supermarket. I mean our trolleys met accidentally once, but oh the froideur that was unleashed. After that, a second instance in the aisle, Pia clicked her tongue when she saw me, and I swear she purposely bumped her trolley into mine. So then I did it to her the following time. I didn't know her name or anything. She was just that annoying person from the supermarket.

In the hormone specialist's waiting room we eyed each other warily. 'No trolley?' I asked. She laughed and asked me what I was doing there. She could probably guess, but instead of going into the gory details of why I was there (bleeding two weeks out of four for no discernible reason, among other things), I said: 'Each night I wake up because my feet are shooting flaming darts at the wall. It keeps me up. When I finally fall asleep, my morning alarm is going off.'

'Just your feet?' She was intrigued. 'Not your whole body? Not your entire body being fed to the universe on the BBQ? Not your breasts in unbearable pain?'

*

This morning she sips her extra-shot large coffee and tells me that when a woman enters the menopause her shamanic qualities come to the fore. Shamanic qualities? I like the sound of this. I sneak a look at Alban, and he starts washing cups in the sink.

On this street, just two shops down from Alban's café is a new Colombian coffee house. Competition for him, he's not pleased. I haven't been there yet. I nudge Pia and lower my voice. 'We should go to the new place to learn to release our shamanic forces. They have quieter tables. Colombian coffee next week?'

'Why wait? Let's go now. We can do our research there.'

We breeze down to the new café. There are hessian sacks filled with coffee beans dotted about. Plants in the corners and on the tables. A different vibe. We order at the till. I ask for lemon-ginger tea, although I'm wondering if real dark hot chocolate is more shaman-like. Pia wants another extra-shot large coffee. We look around for an unobtrusive tucked away table.

I'm hailed by Carla. She's sitting at a table with a friend. Carla is sometimes a guest teacher at the local yoga studio. She conducts the cocoa ceremony and yin yoga and sound baths. I feel her skills are unlimited. She's an uplifting person to be with because she has this habit of smiling widely and speaking in an upbeat tone. Everything is wonderful! How can she be so effervescent ALL THE TIME? I wonder if it ever gets annoying, or cloying, or untrue.

Not to me though, not in the small snatches of time that I see her. I always smile broadly in her company and lose my reticence.

'How are you?' Carla asks. She probably doesn't want to hear every detail of my life but I stage whisper. 'Pia and I are going to release our shamanic selves. As a celebration of being post-menopausal. We are going to pour out the wisdom and kindness in our souls.'

'Reserve some for yourself,' Carla says. Then she speaks seriously. 'You know I'm a healer. I work with the body's chakras. I studied that. That's in your heritage. Why don't you follow that path?'

I'm puzzled. I don't know very much about shamans as yet. I know Carla's heritage is from South America. I remember her telling me she was Brazilian. Pia speaks out what I'm thinking: 'We don't want to learn chakra healing. We are creating rituals for menopause as we couldn't find any. We *will* strengthen and release our inner shamanic forces. Unless you say that it's reserved for people from a specific continent?'

'Oh, no no no,' Carla responds. 'My goodness. The same spirituality, the same powers, different words in different languages. Did you know Korean music is linked to shamanic traditions?'

This is news to me. The world holds so much knowledge that I am clueless about.

'Everything is interconnected,' I say to Carla. 'Some of us feel that instinctively. But many people don't know and don't want to know.'

Carla nods amiably, eyes still sparkling. 'Shamans by different names, all over the world, not just south America. Aboriginal cultures, Tribal people in the Indian subcontinent, First Nation North Americans, I could go on...' She makes a shooing motion with her nimble hands. 'Go on, part-Shamans, have your coffee. Get your flow going.'

Peals of laughter but we can't get mad at her, we have our ritual to perform.

PRE-CONCEPTION CONTRACTS

The cold air stings my face when I step out of Walczak Tower. I stand outside the swooping building, tapping the sole of my burgundy shoe on the pavement, as if deciding which way to go. A taxi glides by, the display strip on its body flashing at me in hot blue. *November 16, 2035* the scrolling text informs me, *21:02 hours*. Then: *Jody Jumps inside the Bridge Box... Three London shows only...* I miss the rest.

My foot taps insistently on the pavement. I am seeking control of myself.

There are some things I am good at controlling. Contracts, computers, print on paper. People. You have to be good at dealing with people to be a successful family lawyer. Although I like to pretend that I'm a dental nurse, especially if I'm out with my mother. She disapproves of what I do. Not that she dislikes the law; it's my specialization which is the problem.

'People drawing up contracts to control each other,' she says. 'I can't agree with that.'

'I'm a pioneer,' I tell her. 'An inventor. And a multi-millionaire.'

'Look what your work has done to you,' she snaps back. 'What kind of life do you have?'

There we stop. She won't believe I like my set-up. She won't believe that my character is so unlike hers. I don't argue. Arguments bore me. I am in command of myself and always have been. Until last week. That kerfuffle has left me unsteady. But at the beginning, I was in control.

*

In June last year, in a soggy marquee at my cousin Jolie's wedding reception, I was introduced to her friend Libby Larsen. Libby, Lena. Lena, Libby. Libby didn't give me a chance to go into my dentist's assistant routine. She pinned me with her arresting blue gaze. 'I've heard of you. I've seen your name in the paper. When there's a famous person brandishing a pre-conception agreement drafted by you and the poor judge has to decide whether the accused spouse is holding up their end of the bargain or not.'

I grimaced. Not all publicity was good publicity. Especially now, when some former clients were ending up in the courts.

'Uh huh.' I tried to change the topic, asking her 'Are you on call all hours like Jolie?' Libby worked with Jolie in Tech Support at a corporate HQ. She didn't answer, instead drawing out from her clutch bag a black-and-cream duo-pho, similar to mine. 'What's your number? I'm being nagged by my boyfriend. I know I'm going to need you soon.'

I gave her my office number, which she inputted on the cream side of her duo-pho. The black side must be for work. Funny; I had chosen black to store my personal protected data and the cream casing for work.

'Were you really the first to draft pre-conceps for couples?' Libby asked.

I nodded. 'The first one I produced was five years ago.

The Planet Spins On Its Axis, Regardless

I was working with Clara Redmond on pre-nups, but when I saw how difficult men were finding it to persuade their partners to have children, I thought this would ease the way. That first document was for a colleague.' I smiled at the memory. 'She could articulate *all* her concerns very clearly, so I had a pretty good template and then I added to it as I went along.'

'So you're doing your bit to stop the birth rate plummeting further.' Libby spoke as if uttering a witticism.

I heard a chuckle behind me. It was Jolie. 'Ask Lena what her mother thinks.'

I didn't reply and Jolie sang, 'Contracts, contracts, what good do they do?'

Libby looked at me with intense interest. 'And your answer?'

'If we can protect our wealth with pre-nups, why can't we safeguard something more important: the welfare of our children? And ourselves? Isn't it better to be prepared for your responsibilities than not?'

'If we are among the lucky few who can create life,' added Jolie. She seemed bent on teasing me because she carried on, 'Do you know that Lena forgot to congratulate me when I told her I was getting married? Instead she reminded me very seriously to bank my eggs and Paolo's sperm.'

Paolo was the baby-faced physicist who had just become her husband. I spied him at the opposite corner of the tent. I left Jolie and Libby having a fit of champagne giggles and headed towards the groom. I may be a secret romantic but I was not going to make a girly display of cackles or tears. I needed male company to offset the bridal vibes.

It was three months later that Libby rang to make a formal appointment with me. 'My boyfriend is mad keen on having a child,' she said. 'He insists we should just try. But really, I need a pre-concep.'

I waited.

'He'll have to do many more child-hours than me,' she went on. 'I want it in writing. Shall I see you alone to put down my terms?'

I gave her the usual advice. 'Firstly,' I said, 'it's better if the agreement is drawn up before you start trying. Some clauses deal with the months of pregnancy. There's even a pre-pregnancy clause about vitamin programmes and such, should you want it. And since this is an *agreement*, you should both be committed to it from the outset. My recommendation is that your boyfriend should be at the discussions.'

That is how I come to have the pleasure of meeting the allegedly impatient father-to-be of Libby's to-be-conceived. Adam Gillick walks into my office and makes my heart thump. He is breathtakingly beautiful.

Libby shakes her duo-pho at me. 'I told you I'd need your number. When you know who the best is, why go anywhere else? Especially when you can afford the best.'

I sense Adam squirming. I hold out my hand and say something welcoming. He starts at my voice. It's husky, like it's scraped past pebbles in my throat. It always surprises people. It doesn't match my too-round cheeks and my long hair, which falls straight to my waist. If my hair doesn't get me a second look, then my voice definitely does.

Clara Redmond, the senior partner at our practice, often ribs me that I have trained my voice to be sexy. 'It always cracks on an important word when you speak, you must have practised that.'

'All natural,' I tell her.

What we get given. Clara has the plaintive 'please, miss' voice of a shy eight year old, the softness of it emerging from her throat a sudden contrast to her stern bony face.

What people like Adam get given. Everything.

I sit at my aluminium desk while Libby and Adam arrange themselves in the chairs opposite. I have plenty of experience in reassuring uncomfortable men. 'This first meeting,' I begin smoothly, 'is just me talking about fairly dull things. I'll give you a rundown of how we put together the agreement. I'll give you a list of all the suggested clauses for you to discuss between yourselves. That usually throws up any issues either of you might have. Those we'll resolve together at the next meetings.'

Clara tells me that when *she* started in pre-nups most men were supremely confident about what they wanted in the contract. The women tended to shrug as if they didn't really want to be there. I hadn't noticed any such difference between the sexes when I started my training. Certainly, in the pre-conception side of things, women are in control. With the current birth rate standing at four births for every thousand people, I can see why they are special; the ones who agree to have children; and even more so, the ones who succeed in doing so.

Clara also tells me that human needs don't change. She may have a point. I've observed that most women do want children, but it's a good ploy to pretend they don't. Oh, how they need to be persuaded. They worry incessantly about micromanaging the future: work, childcare, parent care, their own bodies, the cost of nappy laundry, contractual obligations to save for education, and whom the precious ones belong to, if it comes to that, as it can do.

As if you can predict anything at all. I run my eye over Libby and Adam. I suppose you can predict a few things. This document will not take too long to draft. Here are two charismatic, evenly matched specimens. The only oddness I note is Libby's habit of running her fingers down Adam's thigh to his knee, as if unconsciously stroking feathers. Feathers ruffled by discussion. By the ignominy of sitting in my office?

I see their shadowy outline through the frosted doors as they arrive for the next meeting. Adam's thumb caresses the top of mine as we shake hands. It's a fleeting sensation, like I've imagined it. I react by looking up swiftly into his face. Is that amusement lurking behind his opaque blue eyes? He's just testing, proving he's irresistible. Regaining his power on my turf. I've dealt with one or two charmers like Adam, I know better than to rise to the bait.

'As you know, this agreement sets out in detail the responsibilities and divisions of duty between yourselves, should you have a child. These terms are legally binding, and once signed, are in effect when you're actively working towards a pregnancy.' I pause. 'Let's see how we're doing on the standard clauses. First question, childcare. One of you; other family; or bought services?'

'One of us,' Libby answered.

'Depends on the day,' said Adam.

'Huh?' Libby was surprised.

'What if I have to work?'

'But your time is flexible. You can't take on a lesson if you know you're not free.'

'But I may have to. I may want to. My time is flexible not to suit me but to suit my clients.'

I interject quietly. 'It sounds like you need to make provision for outside help too. Let's return to this later. Let's look at...' I skip the question of financial responsibility for the moment; thinking I know the answer to that.

Then I declare decisively, 'I need five minutes privately with each of you.'

I lead Adam to the small conference room. I ask him if he wants separate representation.

'What do you advise?'

'You only need it if you feel the contract would be unfair. If you are of one mind, it's not required.'

We are sitting adjacent to each other at one end of the egg-shaped table. He pulls his chair forward so his knees touch mine. I can't be sure if this is deliberate. 'I'll stick with you,' he says. 'I'm sure we'll be fine.'

I know I should stay away from this type. 'That's settled then,' I say blandly, letting the file I'm holding brush across his knees as I stand up. He follows me back to my office, walking closer than is strictly decent. I can feel him in my space. But I don't turn around to check, so I can't be too sure, if he's blowing into my hair. There's mischief in his soul. It takes one to recognise one.

I lead Libby to the conference room. I look into her striking eyes, so large and clear. 'You must run through these questions at home,' I insist. 'It's best if the first objection to any clause is aired early on. You'll both have time to think it over by the next meeting. It'll be easier then to reach a compromise.'

'He's a hot head,' Libby says. 'He makes snap decisions. But yes, we'll thrash out some of this before we see you again.'

There is something else I want to mention to the two of them once we are back in the crisp white confines of my office.

'It can be a strain drafting the pre-concep,' I begin delicately. 'Although we recommend it, you need to know that having a contract does not necessarily lead to having a child. With these high infertility rates…' I shrug. There's no legal reason for me to provide this disheartening fact, but I feel obliged to. It rarely stops anyone from proceeding.

Libby brushes aside the comment. 'Oh, Lena, let's sort out the contract and then worry about whether we'll be among the lucky few or not. We've got a good chance. Adam is super fit, you know.'

My desk reflects a distorted image of the super-fit Adam. I sneak a look at the real thing. Tall, broad shouldered. Wavy dark hair. Carries off a bandana. Fine featured. Looks good in polo shirt and baggy shorts. I haven't seen him in shorts, but he's a tennis instructor, so I imagine he spends some of his working life in them. At the moment he's wearing grey casual trousers and a light blue jumper.

'See you in a week or so,' I say, watching them leave. Adam catches my lingering eye. He gives a half smile, a satisfied 'gotcha' expression on his face. We are similar animals. Except he rates higher on the scale of beauty. In my book.

The Planet Spins On Its Axis, Regardless

I am a connoisseur of the stolen moment. I collect these, the moments focused on me, thieving from a time which is not mine, from a story which is not mine. From a man who is not mine. I daisy-chain these moments to make a play to amuse myself. I call it *Preludes and Elusions*.

Sometimes I can't be sure if these delicious momentary encounters really took place or my mind converted a pencil scratch into an ink sketch. I like beginnings. Newness. The start of something. The first locked glances. The first electric touches. That's where my interest lies.

'Beauty is to be admired,' Clara remarks, on the button, walking in as Libby and Adam depart.

'That one knows he's a leopard,' I tell her, 'he flaunts his spots without thinking about it.' She looks at me keenly, but sees I'm grinning.

'They're a sweet couple,' I say. 'This will be over in a few weeks. File closed.'

My desk bleeps thrice: a prompt to call my mother. I click my tongue and re-set the reminder. I'm momentarily distracted from what I was explaining to Libby and Adam, who are leaning back into the white chairs in front of me.

'He's in a huge rush,' Libby says, taking over confidently and talking about Adam as if he wasn't there. 'You'd think the oestrogen in the water has made men develop body clocks. At thirty-six!'

Adam is examining the aluminium floor lamp with a jaded eye. I start again, diplomatically, 'How did you get on with the latest draft I sent?'

'Adam's a bit sick of discussion. But as we've sorted

out the financial responsibilities and the child-hours, he says to just go with the standard format for the rest.'

'Right. Standard terms. Each infidelity will cost one million,' I say cheerfully. I want him to sit up now, but am unprepared for his sudden vehemence.

'This isn't a pre-nup.' His voice is raised. 'What's infidelity got to do with conception?'

'I was joking,' I reply, 'but since you ask the question... plenty.' I glance at Libby who is suppressing laughter. 'Anything can be covered in the pre-concep,' I continue. 'Undesirable behaviour can be curbed for the sake of the child's welfare. Any habits you dislike...' This is one of the ways I amuse myself.

Adam's body stiffens and puffs out. One glance at the rage on his face and I know I have made a mistake. Mentally, I scold myself. Libby lays a calming hand on his arm. 'She's teasing us,' she says. 'Of course, we could put in "the child must have the Gillick cheekbones but not the temper."'

I rush headlong into being serious, hoping to deflect his glower. 'There are just a few points left on which I require your feedback. You two are on a roll; let's tie it up next time.'

It only takes another ten days and we are at our last meeting. There's very little to amend from the recent drafts I'd sent out. We discuss the minutiae, because I'm paid to get that right, for half an hour. Libby excuses herself to use the washroom. I gaze at Adam's image in my desk when something makes me look up.

He's making a moue with his lips. Waiting for a reaction. I'm suddenly conscious that my lipstick is a hot pink. My Schiaparelli party pink. It strikes me that I've been applying a steadily brighter shade of pink with each visit of the Larsen-Gillick couple. I'm embarrassed, but I will brazen it out. I curl my tongue into my mouth behind closed lips, so he can make out that it's a secret smile. I won't let it break out, it will be held in; mine. He leans across the desk and puts his lips close to my right ear. I can't be sure I've heard clearly. It sounds like: 'Luscious pink'. My eyes look up at his, querying. He returns my look innocently. I frown into the distance, betrayed; then I turn my attention to some papers.

When Libby returns I tell them that I'll send out final copies of the document for both of them to sign. I stand up to shake hands. 'Good luck,' I say and funnily, I mean it. It always happens to me at this moment. I want this couple to succeed. Adam squeezes my hand tight, mumbles a 'thank you' and rushes off. He has a coaching appointment.

Libby lingers. 'Care for a coffee?' she asks. 'That underwater café downstairs looked so inviting.'

I hesitate. It's a quarter past three. The meeting has finished earlier than I expected. I don't usually socialise like this, but I accept. 'Yes, that would be nice.' My legal relationship with them is almost over.

We go down to Aquascope on the ground floor. It's situated beneath the swimming pool, entry to which is on the third floor. The bottom of the swimming pool, also the ceiling of the café, is a toughened translucent glass. Hazy shapes of swimmers flutter above us. The wall to the street is clear glass and the other three walls are ultramarine blue. I feel unsteady in here, even when sitting down. It's like having an out-of-body experience. I breathe deeply and focus on the sunburst of yellow coral painted in the centre of the glass table.

Libby launches into amusing gossip about her work and some of our mutual acquaintances, making me laugh. Then she dives into a spate of questions about my work. She is so direct and forceful, it is hard to give guarded replies and I find myself being more honest than usual.

Adam's gloss has a brooding underside, I think to myself, but Libby's brilliance is steadfast. She will be a good mother. I am about to tell her so when I realize it's after four o'clock. 'I must get back now,' I exclaim.

As we walk towards the door Libby asks impishly, 'Is your own pre-concep drawn up ready for when you decide to have children?'

I should brush away this question. Instead I reply with rare candour. 'I don't need a pre-concep.'

'Would you advise that?'

'Let's not talk about what I would advise. Most people want a contract. It makes the game serious. I meant that I don't intend to have a child. So there should be no need.'

Libby looked so baffled that I carried on.

'We legislate for most things, but the law can't predict human behaviour. In everyday life removed from the contract, couples have to find their own logistical and emotional solutions. Sometimes the pre-concep worsens the situation. When it is clearly not being adhered to, one party feels wronged and bitter. Time spent in conflict would be better spent with the child.'

As I speak it dawns on me that having my name bandied about in court is troubling me more than I have admitted.

Libby persists, 'But why no child?'

I sigh. 'I think I know too much. I get all the feedback, after. To improve the agreements, to add in clauses we didn't think about before.' I force a smile. 'I'm of the firm opinion that I will be a sure-shot for post-natal depression.'

Before she can drown me with another 'Why?' I press the lift button.

*

That was last October and I hadn't seen either of them since. I'd asked Jolie how Libby was getting on and the response was 'Fine.' I didn't ask about Adam. But whenever I spotted someone who looked vaguely like him, his face would come sharply into focus. His shoulders, his hands. His hair.

I hadn't thought about his voice. Until last week. I had left late from work after a drinks-do for a colleague from the Macedonia office. I was standing by the lift at the car-charge depot. I had just entered my bay number and put away the swipe card when my arms were gripped from behind. For a second, I felt blind terror.

'Hello, Lena.' It took me a heartbeat to recognise the voice at my neck. My scream was aborted as the voice continued, 'I must speak to you. Now.'

It was Adam who had seized my arms. My handbag dangled from three fingers, which I curled tightly around the strap. My wrenched wrists were held fast against my coccyx. Adam turned me around and started walking me back to Walczak Tower. 'Let's go to your office.'

I struggled to free myself, but was surprised at how physically ineffectual I was. He held my wrists behind me with one hand, and walked by my side, pull-pushing me along. I hadn't managed to articulate any actual words.

'We're going to talk.' The grim set of his lips gave me a sinking feeling.

'My arms... Let go...'

He replied roughly, angrily, 'I'm not letting go till we get to your office.'

I knew I was scared because I had an urge to giggle. It's my default setting when I really don't know what to do.

Adam got the security fob out of my handbag. We took the lift up. He marched me into my office. The lamp came on.

'My arms hurt,' I protested, as he imprisoned them behind me again. He pressed me back into the metal edge of my desk. I squared my shoulders. I would not be cowed by his burning eyes. The next moment he let my left arm go free, but began rattling my body with my right arm, bruising me, swearing at me, with spittle landing on my cheek. I recoiled involuntarily from his name-calling. I couldn't think with my head being shaken off my neck.

'Stop. Please stop.' I realized I was crying. 'Why are you doing this?'

The slamming stopped.

'Why are you calling me a vile bitch?' My voice broke on 'vile.' This was the least hurtful label he'd thrown at me in the space of a minute.

'Didn't you hear me, bitch?' he said. 'It's your fault. And after wasting our time and money.'

'What?' I was still puzzled.

'Libby,' he said, his tone turning nastier still and his face in a snarl, 'has spent all these months *considering* whether to conceive a child. I told her, "If anything in the pre-concep is bothering you, re-draft the damn thing however you want." But no, it's not the contract bothering her. It's the bloody lawyer.'

He put both hands on my shoulders and shook me violently. 'What did you say to her, bitch?'

'I didn't say anything... ' I faltered, finding it difficult to speak. 'Why do you think...'

'Yesterday I had enough of Libby's *considering*.' He loosened his grip again. 'We had an...' he paused. 'I tore up the contract. But guess what Libby said. She said "No point in that anyway. When the expert's experience is that the agreements come to naught after the child is born, and when the expert isn't prepared to get on the child tramline..." '

His hand dug into my shoulder like he wanted my bone to crumble. 'Libby wonders why I begrudge her time to think. *Time to think*. That's what the woman says.' Then he was shouting, 'How can you be an expert when you haven't even had a child?'

'I never claimed to be an expert.' My voice was shaking. 'I just ... made the mistake of... giving my opinion.'

'Who asked for your opinion?' He was still very loud. I hoped someone would hear and come in to see what was going on.

'I honestly didn't mean to put her off the idea.' I felt near to tears again.

He was silent. I stuttered on, 'Believe me, I wasn't giving advice... I was just... answering her questions.'

'So answer this. What were you playing at with me?' This he whispered and held my arm. My skin prickled. He was in my space, his body only two centimetres from mine. I tried to shake free my captive right arm.

'Same as you.'

'You think?'

'I think.'

But I wasn't sure now. I like the sudden surprise of arousal and the dispelling of it, out of necessity. I can go too far, but only for an instant, then I slide back to equilibrium. I don't want to prolong stolen moments; not even into an hour; the ephemerality is the thing. Nothing could be worse than having the object of your lightning fantasy loll around your feet all day.

Adam's game was slightly different. His rules included violence.

'No,' I said. I pushed at him with my free arm, and pulled at his shoulder. 'No. I don't like force.'

'You don't like,' he said, 'Tell me something different, bitch.'

I was squashed back against the desk, he was pressed into me, and there wasn't anywhere to go. For a few seconds, I went limp. I felt his hand on the hem of my skirt, lifting, dragging it up to the top of my thigh. He put his mouth to my ear.

I detected laughter in something he whispered. The laugh woke me, I stamped my heel on his toes through his shoes, he let go of one arm, and I poked two fingers into his eyes.

I escaped to the door, opened it, and ran down the corridor to the next office, slipping into the darkened space. He had followed me to the door, but he wouldn't dare assault me in another office. Would he?

I waited. There was silence. I didn't peep out into the corridor. I smoothed down my hair with my fingers, righted my clothes, and rubbed my arms where the bruises would come up. I heard clicks, unidentifiable small sounds outside. I shivered. Eventually I talked myself into running fast past my office, and to the lift; a sanctuary which came for me no sooner than I had touched the button.

I took it down to the main entrance. I hobbled to the security desk with a conspicuous limp. The guard on duty was a man whom I recognised, but whose name I didn't know. I do, now. His name's Izhar.

'I slipped in the washroom on the seventh floor,' I winced as I spoke, 'and I barely managed to get to the lift. It's so painful. I think I've sprained my ankle.'

I flopped down on a chair. I think I really did look stricken and drained, because Izhar displayed the right degree of concern.

'Do you need a doctor?' he asked, 'or shall I call a cab for you?'

'A cab would be good,' I said, 'but I've left my handbag in my office. Will you be able to bring it down for me please?'

'I can't leave my post, but I can ring security on the fifth. If he comes down to take my place, I could...'

'Whatever. Please arrange it. I don't think I can put any weight on this ankle.' As an afterthought, I said, 'Oh, I hope my client found his way out.'

'The big guy?'

'Yes. He's gone?'

'Yeah 'bout fifteen minutes ago.'

Izhar retrieved my bag while another guard manned the desk. He called me a cab and solicitously put me in it.

In a short while I was in the safety of my home but I couldn't sleep. I was too disturbed. I don't like violence. In any form. I don't like having to resort to it. I hoped I had not damaged Adam's pretty eyes.

I didn't think I could face my office the next day, but I couldn't excuse myself either. I went in but had a quiet day creeping about in my own space except for two meetings. I left early, just as the light was fading. I looked over my shoulder all the way to the car-charge depot. As I approached the car lift, the curly-haired youth in the cubicle, another familiar face whose name I didn't know, slid open the window to call to me. He was angry.

'Your car came down last night,' he said, 'and there was no one waiting to claim it.' Before I could apologise, he went on. 'You're lucky I knew it was yours. I could have let them tow it away. But I used my pass to send it back to your berth. There's a fine slapped on it.'

I thanked him. I explained there had been a sudden emergency and I'd had to return to the office. I drove home.

Strangely, sleep is now a problem. I have a recurring dream in which Adam stalks me. He seizes my arms from behind. He marches me into my office and gives me an earful of abuse. I cry. He calms down. He takes hold of me again, pushes up my skirt. I yield.

In a while the dream will cease, I am sure of it. But now, I loiter outside Walczak Tower in the dark. Straining to hear footfalls behind me.

The air around me remains unruffled. The temper tantrum may have passed, to everyone's relief.

No one will be lolling at my feet, and really, that's how I like it.

THE PLANET SPINS
ON ITS OWN AXIS, REGARDLESS

It's out of your control. Realise this, and everything is easy. Also much more difficult. Because you'll put your efforts in, dial up to the max, then wait. Nothing may happen, something may happen. It's out of your control.

One day you will wake up with the will to eat, and the will to walk, but not the will to care. Take it easy as you go into the new year. Where does it start for you? January? Or some other date that's important to you? Unsolicited advice: select the other date as a re-set date. This is solid advice; it works. Don't join the resolution frenzy in January. Let everyone else turn over a new leaf, watch kindly as they stop drinking alcohol, give up chocolate, take up bouldering. Help them download their fill of health, fitness and mindfulness apps, if you must.

The will to better yourself will return. Feel free to rest until it does. Free yourself this January. Don't tell anyone your re-set date. When pressed for your resolution, say, 'Taking it easy. What about you?'

ACKNOWLEDGEMENTS

Versions of these stories were first published as follows:

'The Unusual Properties of Cork' | *Tongues and Bellies*, Linen Press, 2021

'Three Singers' | produced and broadcast by BBC Radio 4, 2014 | also in *Love Across A Broken Map*, Dahlia Publishing, 2016

'When You Go You Leave A Farce' | *The Mechanics' Institute Review*, 2013

'Tulip Persimmon's Head-Wetting' | *Tongues and Bellies*, Linen Press, 2021

'Where He Lives' | *May We Borrow Your Country*, Linen Press, 2019

'Sweet Peas' | *The Moth* magazine, 2012

'Tipping Point' (a version titled 'Special Delivery') | *Too Asian, Not Asian Enough*, Tindal Street Press, 2011

'A Flash of Pepper' won the Foyles | Haruki Murakami competition, 2012

'Cocoon Lucky' | *Where We Find Ourselves*, Arachne, 2021

'Galvanise Gloss' | *Confluence* journal, 2020

'Shamans in Luburbia' | *Menopause – The Anthology*, Arachne Press, 2023

'Pre-Conception Contracts' (a version titled 'Preludes and Elusions') | *The Mechanics' Institute Review*, 2009

'The Planet Spins On Its Axis, Regardless' | *Visual Verse,* online journal, 2019

ABOUT THE AUTHOR

Kavita A. Jindal is an award-winning fiction writer, poet and essayist. Her novel *Manual For A Decent Life* won the Eastern Eye Award for Literature (2020) and was shortlisted for the Rabindranath Tagore Literary Prize (2022). Her poetry publications include *Raincheck Renewed* and *Patina*. Her short stories and poems have appeared in anthologies and literary journals worldwide and been broadcast on BBC Radio 4, Zee TV UK and European radio stations. Selected poems have been translated into Arabic, German, Italian, Punjabi, Romanian, Spanish and Ukrainian. She previously served as Senior Editor at *Asia Literary Review* and is the co-founder of *The Whole Kahani* collective for British-Asian writers. She enjoys collaborating with other artists across a range of projects. www.kavitajindal.com